Out of The Woods

Taylor Rogers

GoldFinch Books LLC

Out of the Woods

Copyright © 2023 by GoldFinch Books LLC

All rights reserved.

ISBN 979-8-988933-0-1

No portion of this book may be reproduced in any form without written permission from the publisher or author, except in the case of brief quotations embodied in critical articles and reviews.

NOTE: This is a work of fiction.

Names, characters, places, and incidents are a product of the author's imagination. Any resemblance of actual persons, places, events, businesses or locales are coincidental.

For questions please reach out to GOLDFINCH Books Llc

Dedication

This book is dedicated to my family who have supported and encouraged me throughout the entire process of this book and life. Without them this book would not be in existence, and I would just like to take a moment to thank each of them.

I want to thank my mom who introduced me to my love of reading and books, for being my first editor and for being the person who first thought I could do it and be a writer.

I want to thank my dad for introducing me to the great outdoors. Sitting on the hillsides with him where we hunted was where I first came up with the idea for this book.

And I want to thank my sister for her constant support and for lovingly pushing me to finish this book.

I love you all!

Prologue

My body feels weightless, similar to the feeling you get when jumping on a trampoline. You know that split second when you're at the top of a jump, hanging suspended in the air. The freeing sensation of your hair floating all around you, arms reached out to the sides, welcoming the weightlessness. The exact moment, right before gravity reaches up and snatches you back down to the spring-lined black mesh, only to start the whole process over again. That's what this feeling is. Like I am floating, waiting for the crash as a soft, reassuring voice murmurs in my ear. This state of semi consciousness keeps me awake just enough to make small sense of the world around me. I am able to make out slight shapes and shadows passing in front of my eyes. That, along with my muddled memory, causes some things to start to make sense.

I am surrounded by trees, hundreds of them. The constant motion in my vision along with the weightlessness and the calming voice, confused me at first. My brain is so muddled that it takes several heartbeats for me to realize I am being carried through the woods. And now that I realize it, the trees look kind of funny, almost like they are growing sideways. The ground must have a grade, so either we are climbing some kind of hill, or I am really out of it. Each has an equal shot of being accurate. As we, me and the murmuring voice carrying me continue, the ground starts sloping more, and other sounds become noticeable. At first, they sound a good distance off, but gradually they get closer and closer. I should have recognized them as sirens from emergency vehicles, road noise from cars on the highway, and the sound of many voices. But my brain isn't able to process any of this. Every sound simply goes in one ear, rattles around in my head as if it were hollow, and exits out the other ear.

The sky is dark and stormy when my carrier and I finally break through the trees. Rain patters on my face, stinging my cheeks before rolling down my skin into my hair. The voices I had noticed earlier grow louder, but they register exactly the same.

"We're almost there, Chloe," the soft voice says.

Wait a minute… I heard that. The voice; it is no longer just a muttering sound, but the voice of a man. And a voice I recognize. Some small part of me seems to come awake. An overwhelming amount of emotions flood through me as the realization of what is happening comes back. A twinge of panic shoots through my chest, and I can feel my heartbeat quicken with it. I can't feel anything outside my basic senses. I'm sure even if I tried to show some sign of acknowledgment to the voice and turn my head, I wouldn't be able to. All I can do is stare at the trees as they slowly move by.

The constant motion is starting to make me dizzy. The fogginess is starting to creep back in and as it does, a new fear makes its way in with it. What happens if the darkness takes me under again? Will I wake up next time? Tears sting the corners of my eyes as the world starts to fade in and out slowly. Noises that were once getting louder start to dull again. Flashing lights that were reflecting on the black trees start to disappear as the blackness works its way toward the center of my vision. My earlier sense of becoming alert is quickly slipping from me. I try to grab ahold of it, but my mind is hazy, thoughts confusing with others. I'm not even sure if we are moving anymore when a familiar face appears above mine…

And that is the last thing I remember before my vision goes black.

Chapter One

Chloe

This summer flew by faster than any other in my memory. The last summer before real life began, adult life. Somehow, it feels different knowing that I wouldn't be buying books and supplies and heading back to school this fall. Back to the structure of having every hour of your day planned for you by someone else. The thought of it now being completely up to me was daunting. Yes, the structure of the work would be the same, but still, the library had been easy. Put books away, check people out, and help them with any questions they had. But that was ending soon too, at the end of the summer. The weeks have gone by so swiftly that the first hints of fall were already starting to creep in, just the tips of the leaves were transitioning from their summery green to faint warm orange. I can see it now on the leaves of the tree outside my boyfriend Chris's dining room window.

This was my last summer of blissful leisure, and after weeks of brutal finals, I had earned it. I had decided after graduation I would keep my part-time library assistant job through the summer as a sort of wind down before officially putting my new English degree to work. Thanks to a 4.0 GPA and a glowing review from my boss at the library, I will officially start my job as a paralegal at one of the law firms in town in just a few short weeks. It would certainly be a change of pace, but I was ready.

I pull my attention from the window back into the apartment and study the expressions of the others in the room. The other three chairs are occupied by Chris and his two best friends and fellow paramedics- Bill and Fred. The light from the window beside me casts across the table just enough to throw a golden light across Chris's hair. People often joked that we were meant to be together because we look so similar, and I can see it if I don't look closely. Both of us are tall and lean from growing up playing sports. My white- blonde hair and icy-blue eyes showed my Norwegian heritage, which complimented

Chris's sandy-blond surfer cut and dark blue eyes. But I always felt if you looked close enough, his hair looked like pure gold, which in comparison, made my lightness look completely washed-out. His eyes are such a dark blue they don't even seem natural, while mine are so pale I always have to make sure I have sunglasses with me just so I can open my eyes outside.

He glances up at me and those blue eyes twinkle as he smiles; no doubt, he noticed me staring. I smile back as he refocuses on what we are doing. The three men all have the same studious expression as they look down on the map sitting on top of the small wooden table.

"Okay, we're thinking of going up a bit farther than what we had originally talked about," Bill says, pointing to a spot on the map. As the only one of us who has ever been on this trail before, Bill has taken the leadership role in this planning process. When not in uniform, Bill is always wearing the newest Patagonia gear and climbing any new trail he can find. Even now in his work gear, his darkly tanned skin is a dead giveaway that he spends a lot of time outdoors. Not to mention his short dark hair always has the faint markings of his favorite baseball cap.

"We were hoping to take the path that passes Sunfish Pond and goes straight to the high point of the mountain. That's the most scenic view, but it's also the path that sucks the most to climb." He leans back in his chair and looks around at us all, flicking crumbs from the earlier pizza off his uniform. All three of them had been so excited to get started with our final decision-making meeting that they had come over immediately after their shift to work out the fine details. Of course, after our small meeting, they would turn right back around and go straight to the station to work a double-shift a few hours later. The guys were all hard working, picking up extra shifts and pulling double duty so they could all get the time off together for our trip.

I showed up shortly after they had. I had thankfully agreed to pick up dinner on my way home from Chris's for my mom and siblings because the earlier mentioned pizza had been demolished within minutes of its arrival.

"That's cool. Then we can camp at the pond over night; they have some spots where people can set up tents and a couple of fire pits if we get there early enough," Chris points out.

"Okay. When will we start out?" I ask again for what feels like the thousandth time. Every time we nail that part down, something would happen and the date would be up in the air once again. The last time we had tried to nail down a date, Martha, Bill's girlfriend, had to work, so that pushed it back. And then the time before that, the boys couldn't get the time off work, and so on until now our mid-summer trip had become an end of summer trip.

"We're thinking Sunday morning so we can get an early start, and we thought of coming back maybe Thursday afternoon," Fred chimes in and leans back in his seat, the chair creaking. His coppery red hair flashes in the sunlight streaming in as he looks around at us. His brown eyes always seem to have a mischievous glint in them that makes me think he's always up to something.

"Cool, sounds like a plan," I say, sliding my chair back from the table and standing. "Well, I have to get going; my mom wants me to pick up dinner on my way home." I lean down and give Chris a kiss, earning a gagging sound from Fred. I give him a quick finger gesture as my good-bye before waving at Bill on my way out.

Our small town of North Bend, Washington, is nestled away in the foothills of the Cascade Mountain range. The hiking trails, camping areas, and a very popular outlet mall give us enough tourism to not completely melt into the surrounding forests. But this is the kind of town where everyone knows everyone.

For dinner, I drive to one of the few restaurants we have in town and walk in to order some food to-go. Pushing the glass door open, I start out to my car, juggling a large carton of home-style fried chicken, my keys, and a large drink when I hit something hard, spilling the drink and landing on my butt while luckily keeping a grip on the food.

"You all right?" a familiar gruff voice asks. Looking up, I brush a strand of my hair that has fallen into my eyes and take in all six-foot, four inches known as Tom Knight.

I have known Tom since kindergarten. Together, we sat through many sports' assembly meetings together due to him being the captain of the football team, and I was the captain of the cross-country team. We had gotten to know each other pretty well during those years. Tom was every bit of the golden boy, small-town football player you see in all the movies - tall, strong, smart, and all around one of the most genuine people you would ever meet. But like most people, we drifted apart after high school. Even though we both had gone to the same college, we had majored differently taking us to opposite sides of the campus.

"Yeah, sorry," I say, feeling totally embarrassed. "I wasn't paying attention to where I was going." I can feel the warmth of my blush creep on my cheeks.

"That's okay. Here, let me help you." He chuckles, reaching a hand down.

"Thanks."

I bend back down to pick up my fallen keys when the now empty pop cup catches my eye. The distinct color of wet cement around a pair of gray shoes speckled with dark spots makes my heart drop deep into my chest. I flash my gaze up and take in Tom's shirt, which is now completely soaked with Cherry Cola.

"I'm so sorry; I got you all wet!" I gasp, shocked at my own clumsiness. He grabs the edges of his shirt to pull it away from his body, and I grab some of the napkins from my bag that I had shoved in there from earlier in the restaurant and start dabbing at his chest.

"It's no big deal; really, it's just soda. It will come right out." But he still grabs some of the napkins from my hands and rubs at the wet spot on his shirt. "So, how's your summer been? Got any plans now that we've graduated?" he asks nonchalantly.

I snort, same old Tom. Always the one to try to make a shitty situation a positive one. "It's been pretty good; Chris and I are planning to go hiking next week with a couple of friends. How about you?" I ask while searching for more napkins.

"I've been lifeguarding and was one of the head counselors at the kid's summer camp over at the community center. I get to be in charge of the water sports and recreation. I actually found out right before graduation that I was accepted into the University of Washington's physical therapy program, so I will be heading up there in about a month."

"Oh my god!" I exclaim, gesturing toward him with my handful of soggy napkins. "That's so amazing! Congratulations." As well as being extremely kind and amazingly athletic, Tom is also incredibly smart.

He nods in thanks, which brings his attention back down to his shirt again. "You know what? I think the shirt is a lost cause; I'll just wash it when I get home." He pulls the napkins from the soiled shirt with a sigh

"You sure? I would be happy to pay to get it washed or buy you a new one." A guilty feeling keeps washing over me. Of all the people to run into, it had to be the nicest guy in town.

"Yeah, it's fine, Chloe. Really, it's not that big of a deal."

Still feeling ashamed, I turn to my car mere steps from where I totally humiliated myself and unlock the doors to pile my bag and the chicken into the passenger seat.

"Well, I guess I will see you around then. I should probably get home before I dump the chicken on the next unsuspecting person. And sorry again about the shirt." I gesture toward his chest and the obvious stain.

"It's fine, I promise." He smiles and waves the gesture away. We say our goodbyes, and he turns and walks down the street. I jump in my car, feeling totally humiliated and wishing I had dumped the soda down my own shirt. I watch Tom until he rounds the corner, out of sight. Slowly, I turn on my car and head home.

Chapter Two

Chloe

When I walk in the front door, my four-year-old sister Lilly is running down the hallway and through the living room, screeching that she doesn't want a bath, while my mom is chasing behind. I slide the chicken onto the counter and head to my room, rolling my eyes as I pass my teenage brother Ethan's room. I can hear the pounding of hard rock music behind a door covered in 'no trespassing' signs. When I reach my room, I shut the door and pull out the large hiking backpack I had bought for this trip from the top of my closet and throw it onto the bed. Moving to my dresser, I start pulling out clothes and tossing them next to the bag. I had just tossed my third shirt and was debating between which two pairs of jeans I wanted to pack when there was a soft knock on my door.

"Come in," I yell over the deep bass from the room next-door, while continuing to toss clothes everywhere.

"Hey, honey, do you need any help?" my mom semi-shouts. She must have given up on the bath for tonight and left Lilly to her own devices. Before I can answer, she is already heading to the bed and begins folding the clothes.

"Thanks." I hand her the pairs of pants I had decided on and start putting the other pair back.

"So, where are you guys headed?" she asks.

"Same place we decided on before. We are going to stop at the pond the first night then head over to the high point and stay at a camp ground for the rest of the trip." I move over to my sock drawer and start digging for my wool socks. Though the weather should be mild, I don't want to regret not packing them. One thing you learn when growing up in the Pacific Northwest is that weather, and especially mountain weather, can change quickly.

"So, who all is going?" she asks in a typical mom *'I don't want to sound like I'm prying, but I really am,'* kind of way.

"Um, well, me, of course, and Chris. His friends Bill and Fred and their girlfriends Martha and Carly are coming, too. You know Carly; Chris and I graduated with her. She's the one who came to dinner with us after graduation, the one wearing the bright pink dress."

"I didn't know Carly and Fred were that serious," she comments and helps me put the rest of the clothes into the bag.

Carly and Fred got close after meeting a few times at mutual friends' parties and get togethers. They have only been officially dating for a few months now.

"Well, yes and no. Fred wanted to invite her to come along but didn't want it to feel super awkward so we all agreed to pack two tents and to split it up boys and girls. I guess it works out for the best, one less tent to haul up and down the mountain, and I don't have to listen to Chris snore." My mom snorts as she zips up my bag which is now fully packed with all the clothes, I feel I will need and most of my general supplies. I'm just waiting on a few more items to show up from Amazon and then I'll be all set.

I wander back to the kitchen and grab a piece of chicken. I pass the remnants of a half-eaten drumstick at the dine-in bar on one of Lilly's princess plates. I move to the living room and plop on the couch, exhausted from the day of work, followed by running errands and planning for our trip. My mom follows after dipping into Lilly's room to tuck her in. She grabs a chicken breast along with two plates. She hands one to me as she moves to the chair across the room. I start switching through the T.V. channels until I settle on one of those teen reality shows my mom calls 'trash T.V.,' but I secretly find them amusing. I crank the volume up to try to drown out the slow thud of Ethan's music.

A door creaks open and a sudden blast of music fills the house, then cuts off. I look up and Ethan is stalking toward the kitchen, his long dark hair partially covering his face and his baggy clothes make it look like he suddenly lost two hundred pounds. "It lives," I say in mock terror as he passes me.

"Shut up!" he snaps and shoves my feet off the coffee table.

"Hey now, you two knock it off. And Chloe, turn the volume down before you wake Lilly; I just got her down." My mom sighs, obviously aggravated.

I nibble my chicken leg till there's not much left but bone. I toss the remote to my mom and follow Ethan to the kitchen. I hear the channel switch to the news, and the weather-man starts talking about possible showers throughout the next couple of weeks.

"So, how's Tanya?" I ask.

"She's fine," he grumbles. Tanya is my brother's psychotic Goth girlfriend who enjoys piercings, spider web tattoos and definitely not me.

"Cool. Has she tried to suck anyone's blood yet?" I chuckle and grab another piece of chicken.

"For the last time, she's not a vampire," he snaps and sits on a barstool, tearing into a thigh piece.

"No, but she wants to be," I counter and dump the bones of my devoured pieces of chicken into the garbage. I leave the kitchen before he can think of a comeback. On my way back to my room, I earn a look of disapproval from my mom, but I ignore it.

I pass the row of family pictures in the hall and stop to look at the last one. The people in the picture looked happy, well except for Lilly, who was just a baby. It was one of those silly staged mall photos where everyone is all coordinated and super posed, but we were a whole family then. My mom was holding Lilly in her arms with Ethan and me on either side; Ethan looking like his happier, short-haired self. And there in the back was my dad, beaming at the camera like it was the happiest day of his life. Little did we know, it would be the last picture that would show us all together. A few months after it was taken, my dad was hit by a drunk driver on his way home from work; he died instantly. I can still remember that night… I can still hear the police-man knocking on the door, followed by my mom's sobs echoing from the doorway.

Besides my mom, Ethan had taken my father's death the hardest out of all of us. After the accident, he became different, and gone was the happy, soccer-loving thirteen-year-old. He started growing his hair long, wearing baggy clothes, not talking to anyone, and dating Tanya. Lilly had just been a baby, so she doesn't remember him. I missed my dad a lot, but I am not sure if I miss him or who I wished he had been more. He had always been working when Ethan and I were younger, and that was something that always bothered me. He would leave before we woke and didn't get home until we were already in bed. On the one-off weekends when he was home, it was odd because he would 'play' parent, ordering us around and getting frustrated when we didn't listen to him. He always expected us to be the kids we weren't… but I guess I always wished he was the parent he hadn't been.

Our relationship became even more strained when Lilly was born. To him, she wasn't an *oops* baby late in life; she was his second chance. He had spent more time with her in the few months after she was born than he had spent with me in my whole life. He was home almost every weekend, and during the week, he made sure he was always home in time to help put her to bed. But even with him home more, his attention was wholly invested on Lilly. There were still lots of soccer games, cross-country meets, and other events where Ethan and I would look into the stands and just see Mom cheering us on, since Dad always volunteered to stay home with Lilly. His excuses ranged from the times of our events being too close to naptime or there being too much sun or too many people. It seems silly to me now that he is gone that I was jealous of the relationship he had with a baby, especially knowing she will never get to actually spend time with him or really know him. The only relationship she will have with him is from the stories we tell her. Despite all of that, I had never felt anything but love for my sister. Even with my dad acting as he did, it was never her fault. Even goth-punk Ethan can't resist Lilly's charm. The whole family is putty in her chubby hands. And I do wish my dad was still around, even if just for her to be able to know just how much he loved her.

I sigh and continue down the hall, and once I reach my room, I throw myself on my bed and lay there, looking at the ceiling for several minutes. Staring at the off-white ceiling always seems soothing and is the best way to let my brain reset. Something about the simpleness of the color mixed with just giving my mind a chance to unwind and organize my thoughts always makes me feel better. After laying there long enough that I feel like it's too much of a waste of time, I get up and pull my laptop out. I start googling the Sunfish Pond area, and the pictures I am finding are all so beautiful. The forest, from the trees to the small plants, is filled with such rich, green colors. The pond itself looks like something you would see on the front of a brochure. The water is so crystal-clear, you could actually see the clouds in the sky reflecting across its surface.

Another bonus I see when flipping through the images is the terrain looks easy enough to hike through. I come across a picture from someone's travel blog and see a snap shot of one of the camping spots. The sky above the traveler's tent is dark gray and stormy, the grass glistening from the rain. The photo reminds me of the predictions the weather man had made on the news earlier. I open a new window in my browser and do a quick search for the forecast next week. He had been right; the chances of rain early on in the week are nearly one hundred percent, but it looks like it is supposed to clear up. I reach for my phone and dial Chris' number, who answers after the second ring.

"Hello?" his voice echoes slightly, like he is in a very large room. Looking at the clock, I see it's already eight and I know he's already started his second shift at the station.

"Hey. I don't mean to bother you at work, but I just checked the weather, and it looks like it's going to rain on and off for almost the entire time we are up there." I scroll down to find the precipitation map and click play to see if there's a chance the rain skirts the trail we are planning to take. I hear Chris mumble something to people in the background.

"Yeah, Bill says he saw that and decided to just bring some extra tarps. Just pack for it. I don't think any of us want to push it back again," he says with a frustrated undertone.

I'm about to respond when someone shouts something in the background that I don't quite catch, but I clearly hear Chris holler back, "I'm not telling her that!"

"You're not telling me what?" I chuckle, curious as to not only who was speaking, but what was said that Chris was so resistant to share with me.

"Nothing. Trust me, you don't want to know what Fred just said." He chuckles. I'm about to press the matter further when a series of beeps goes off in the background. "Hey, I have to go, but I will talk to you later. Okay?"

"Yeah, no, that's fine. Go. Be safe! I love you."

"Always. I love you, too," he responds before the line goes dead.

I look down at my phone and see my background. It's a photo of Chris and me at the pumpkin patch last year. It is totally basic, but I love it. We had started dating when we met our freshman year of high school. We sat next to each other during home room and we've been inseparable ever since. He has always been there for me. When my dad died, he was there for whatever I needed. He brought meals over, watched Lilly when my mom, Ethan, and I had to plan the funeral, and sometimes he'd just sit on my bed and hold me while I cried. He was there, no matter what.

Not to say our relationship was one-sided; I have always been there for him, too. Chris didn't have a very good relationship with his parents, so just like we had planned, I showed up at their house the day he turned eighteen and helped load all his stuff into our cars. We spent his birthday eating pizza on boxes and moving him into the apartment he had lined up months prior. We had been through a lot together and have learned to make every day count, and that's why I love the simple photo of us sitting on a hay bale at a pumpkin patch.

I go back to scrolling around on the internet until almost midnight. After I turn the lights off and stow my computer back into its hiding spot, because Lilly is destructive to anything she finds out. I strip off my jeans and T-shirt and pull-on Chris's fire academy sweatshirt that I love to sleep in. I crawl under the covers in my bed, the pounding of Ethan's music still echoing through the house as I drift off to sleep.

Chapter Three

Chloe

Sunday morning finally comes, and I am finishing up packing the last few things, like my toothbrush and hairbrush. My mom continuously comes in with items she thinks I will need. Several of them I am able to talk her out of, like my winter jacket or her big black umbrella, but somehow, many other items make it into the bag like the scarf and hat set my grandparents had gifted me two Christmases ago, yet still had the tags on them, as well as several extra pairs of wool socks. Thankfully, Chris came to my rescue around ten to pick me up. Though even he left with the afore mentioned umbrella, which was pushed in his hand by the mother hen.

Once all my things are packed away in Bill's van, I hug my mom and sister goodbye, though

Mom still asks if I have everything, even after I was already in the car, the umbrella swiftly hidden beneath the seat after Chris slides the car door shut. I settle into the middle bench seat with Chris. Martha and Carly were already in the back seat, chatting up a storm. Bill slides into the driver's seat, and Fred is seated next to him.

"Alright, everybody ready?" Bill asks, half turning in his seat to get a look at all of us. He gets a chorus of yeses, starts the van, and pulls away, officially starting the two-hour drive toward the base of the mountain.

I rifle through my bag, looking for my camera, when Chris bends down and snags the scarf. He chuckles and folds it up. "I love your mom; only she would insist you pack a scarf in the summer." He places it back into the bag still smiling.

"I love how you know it was her and not me." I laugh, sitting back up, having successfully fished the camera out.

"Well, that's because in all the years I have known you, I don't think I have seen you wear a scarf once."

I smile, then start taking pictures of the scenery. We are going through older farm areas as fields of grass and trees and long-forgotten barns fly by the windows. Eventually, I get bored and turn the camera toward the people in the car. I get a couple of Martha and Carly without them noticing, and then some of Fred and Bill, with Bill making faces in the rearview mirror. I also get some of Chris staring out the window, his hair highlighted by the sun streaming in through the glass, but his blue eyes are shadowed. Finally, I get Fred to take one of the two of us. When I run out of things to take pictures of, I put the camera away and lay my head on Chris's shoulder and stare out the window. Soon the countryside flying past turns into dense forest.

We eventually pull off the highway and travel down a small gravel road, and my seatbelt tightens as I bounce with the van when it hits a particularly deep pothole. Several *oofs* echo from the others and Bill slows down slightly before easing the van into another one. The gravel roads eventually opens up into a small parking lot with signs indicating the start of the trail. When we finally stop, the boys hop out and start unpacking the tarps, bags, and tents. I go back to taking pictures, only this time of the big mountain that looms in front of us. I notice the temperature has dropped several degrees now that the mountain is blocking out the sun.

I slowly wander over to one of those informational signs the state puts up that talks about the flora and fauna you may come across. The black and white images recall memories of a book I had purchased for this trip, perhaps the one thing left in my room I meant to bring and accidentally left on my bookshelf. I scan through the sign and come to the section about the wildlife in the area. There are a lot of different small animals mentioned like deer, rabbits, snakes, and insects you might see. Then it shifts to the larger animals, like wolves, cougars, and bears. After scanning it, I meander back to the group. The girls move to pick their bags up from the ground, still chatting away. Chris walks over to me holding my bag in his hands.

"Learn anything?" he asks while helping me slip the bag onto my shoulders. Its weight settles on to my back, and I adjust its positioning with my hands. Luckily, I had the forethought to put all my heavy items in the bag and practiced walking around with it so I could grow accustomed to the weight of it.

"Yeah, actually. I learned about the kind of insects that are up here. We brought bug spray, right? And did you know there are bears and cougars up here?"

"Yes, we brought plenty of bug spray, and I heard something about black bears up here, but they are small and tend to live down farther in the forest than where we are camping. We will still have to be super careful with where we put the food, though. And usually, if you make enough noise, cougars stay away, and with those two," he jabs his thumb toward the other two girls, "we should be just fine."

I nod, but the feeling of having something that dangerous so close is creepy. Chris hooks one of the tents and a sleeping bag to the top of my backpack, and I lean against the van, watching as Carly tries to carry her bag, one of the tents, a sleeping bag, and a purse. Finally, Fred notices his struggling girlfriend and helps hook the sleeping bag on her backpack and helps get it on her back. Once she's settled, he tucks her purse under one of the van seats, out of sight, before Bill locks the van with an assuring beep. The tent he tries to attach to his bag, which already has his gear and one of the food bags nearly causes everything to dump onto the ground. Needless to say, it takes a few minutes and some strategic placement of gear before we actually get going.

A small foot trail sits at the very base of the mountain, and we find that makes a good starting point. Eventually, we divert from it and move onto another worn path that has a small wooden sign indicating a more direct route to the pond.

We have been hiking for a couple of hours when we finally decided to take a break.

"Here seems as good a place as any," huffs an out of breath Bill.

We all set our packs down with a big *thump* and start rubbing the kinks in our shoulders. I move to sit on a fallen log and rub my shoulders. *So much for all those practice walks with the bag.* Chris follows and sits next to me, avoiding several knobs where branches had snapped off.

"It feels nice being out here." He takes a deep breath and peers at me from the corner of his eye.

"Yeah, it's quiet and so pretty." I look around, trying to soak in as much of the calm feeling the forest seems to exude.

I gaze around and spot a pair of birds on a branch take off and chase each other through the trees until they disappear into a set of shrubs. A loud *snap* catches me off guard, and startled, I whip my head to see Chris has broken off one of the bigger branches from the log and is now stripping the little twigs attached to it with his pocketknife.

"Here you go," he says, handing me the now smooth stick with an accomplished grin on his face.

"A walking stick." I smile. "Thanks." I lean in and kiss him, then stand to see how well it works. It feels sturdy and actually a pretty good height. There is another *snap*, and I turn to see Chris now deeper in the trees, snapping off a tree limb similar to mine, except taller and slightly thicker. He turns and grins as he weaves back to me through the brush. I laugh and reach for his hand, grabbing it as we walk back to the rest of the group.

"It should be another hour or so before we reach the pond," Fred is saying when we reach the group. A chorus of small groans escapes a few of our mouths at the thought of still having to hike uphill for any amount of time.

Fifteen minutes later, our packs are all loaded back up and we start hiking back up another small game trail we find, leading toward the pond.

Chapter Four

Chloe

The pond is even more beautiful in person than the photos I had seen online. The water is crystal-clear, reflecting the sky and clouds perfectly. Tall cattail plants grow in large patches all around the perimeter, and there is a grassy clearing next to the pond used for camping.

"Oh, look!" Carly gasps, pointing across the field. On the shoreline closest to us, we spot a couple of fellow hikers who are busy pitching their tent. But that wasn't what had grasped our group's attention. On the opposite side of the lake, we see a small family of deer grazing on the tall grass. A buck with an impressive set of antlers stands closer to the tree line, though not quite as bold as the three does who strayed near the water. They make such a beautiful picture, and even the other hikers stop making camp to watch them. At one point, one of the does lifts her head and glances our way. She doesn't seem nervous by our presence, just curious. I could have even sworn she made direct eye contact with me, but I blink in surprise and her head was back down, pulling another mouthful of grass by the time I looked again.

Eventually we break our trance, and we notice the sun has dipped below the tree line and we still needed to set up camp for the night. We set our tents closer to the tree line to give the other hikers space, but we still got here early enough to secure one of the spots with a fire pit. We unpack the two tents and quickly set them up and after a quick discussion, decide to throw tarps over each just to be on the safe side. After our bags are stowed in the tents and the sleeping bags are unrolled Fred, Chris, and Carly go in search of fire wood while Bill, Martha, and I stay to watch camp and prepare dinner. I glance around and give the tent poles one more good check before standing to help get dinner started. As I straighten, I glance across the lake just in time to see the deer wander back into the trees and disappear.

"This has been so much fun so far," Martha says while unloading cans of chili from one of the food bags. "I love hiking; I find it so peaceful"

"Yeah," I answer, finally looking away from where the deer went. "I have been waiting for this trip for so long."

I open each can and hand them over for Martha to dump into the pot, which is sitting in wait for the fire. We work in companionable silence that comes from knowing each other for years. Soon, we hear the others come stomping back through the trees each with an armful of dead branches. "Nice work, guys," I comment and crack open a bag of biscuits that had been baked beforehand.

Once the fire is started, we hang the pot over the flames with special hooks that Fred stuck into the ground. Martha stands watch over the food, making sure it doesn't burn while the rest of us roll a few nearby logs to set up as benches. Happy chatter echoes through our camp while we work, then a relaxed ease settles over us as the sun slowly sinks behind the trees. Once dinner is served, all conversation slowly dies, everyone too focused on eating.

"What time are we getting up tomorrow?" Carly angles her spoon and scrapes the bottom of her bowl to get the last little bit of food. I look around at the others, curious about the answer, too.

"Probably around sunrise," Chris answers, looking around to see if anyone objects. The group remains silent, and Bill simply nods in agreement.

"How hard is the hike going to be?" I ask, getting up to gather everyone's small, collapsible bowls and utility fork, spoon, knife hybrids. Chris stands and pulls a map from his nearby backpack. Unrolling it on the stump we used as a prep table for dinner, he studies it, tracing his finger along the trail we used to get here. Bill gets up and joins him.

"Well, it will be harder… A lot of it is mostly uphill as we get nearer to the top, but there are a couple different trails we can take." I peer over Chris's shoulder while fishing the small bottle of dish soap out of my bag.

"That one looks easier," I say, pointing to one that looks like a straight shot to the top of the mountain. I hear a laugh as Fred comes up to look at the map.

"Not unless you're a mountain goat; that trail has an almost ninety-degree incline. That's only for the really hard-core hikers and forest rangers. I think we should use this one." Fred points to a trail that curves and zigzags in places, and Bill nods again in agreement.

"It will be a little easier. The incline is gradual, and the only main concern is the trail is narrow and it's been a while since I have taken it. I'm not sure the shape it's in now, but you never know…" he says with a shrug. We all agreed on Bill and Fred's trail right when the first drops of rain splatter onto the map.

Chapter Five

Chloe

Luckily, we had already put tarps over the tents, because after stringing up the rest of the food into the trees and a quick cleanup of camp the rain came, fast and strong. We reach our tents just before we get totally soaked. Looking out the door of the tent, the rain falls in a solid gray sheet against the nearly black sky, giving the impression of a waterfall engulfing the tent. With the light from our lantern, I can see small streams of water trailing down the blue nylon sides, creating small patterns. As soon as the girls and I get in and zip the door closed, we quickly take off the wet clothes and change into our dry pajamas. With our sleeping bags and backpacks in here with us, there is very limited space, but we do our best to lay out the damp outer layers of our outfits to give them a chance to dry for tomorrow.

"I thought the rain was supposed to wait till Tuesday," I yell toward the boys' tent, which is just a few feet away.

"I guess it changed its mind," Fred hollers back. I smile and shake my head, and I hear Carly giggle behind me.

"Well, what do you want to do now?" I ask, turning toward the girls.

"Oh, I brought Mad Libs!" Carly offers as she digs through one of the many bags stored in our tent. She keeps brushing her curly hair out of her face as it is just slightly too short to be pulled up into a pony tail, and she already removed her headband to give it a chance to dry. When she finally produces the little flip book, we play a couple of rounds, which produces many laughs and a few shouts from the boys' tent to be quiet. According to several of our games, Fred was going to marry a goat on the moon in the summer, Bill is going to harvest mangos on a dreary Friday night during the eclipse, and Martha is now a cat walker for a rich seamstress in London. Needless to say, it was a really entertaining game, and it was fun to hangout with just us girls. Normally, we only ever hang out in a big group.

When we finally decide to go to sleep, it takes some shuffling around to make enough space for three people to lie down. We had originally planned to pile the gear in the middle and sleep around the edges of the tent, but with the rain, we have to keep everything as far from the edge as we can, so it won't allow water to drain in and completely soak everything. I end up with my backpack under my pillow, and Carly all but slept on top of most of the other bags. The rain is almost falling too hard to be soothing, and I lay there for close to an hour, wondering if I will ever fall asleep. But it must have eventually lulled me into unconsciousness because before I knew it, there is rain in my dreams.

Chapter Six

Chloe

I hear the chirping of birds when I wake up, and there is a distinct absence of pounding rain from outside the tent. I roll over and see two lumps in sleeping bags still sound asleep. I smile when the one containing Martha snorts. I reach under my pillow and pull my backpack into my lap. I slowly start pulling out clothes and get dressed before trying to brush my teeth with my hydro flask water bottle, I had the foresight to fill and put by my sleeping bag. When I slowly unzip the tent, the amount of sunlight that hits my face momentarily blinds me. The grass around the campground glistens from thousands of individual raindrops that stuck to everything from all the rain and the morning sunshine. The scene of the campground looks like it came right out of one of Lilly's fairy books. I glance down to watch my step and find a small stream flowing around the tent like a tiny moat. Carefully, I step over it and walk across the camp, dodging several large mud puddles before reaching Chris and Bill, who are crouched at the fire pit that is now a slopping mud hole. "Morning," I greet them and bend to give Chris a kiss.

"Morning, Chloe," Bill mumbles, and Chris reaches up to grab my hand and slowly stands. I lean against him; his body heat helps fight the morning chill.

"I see leaving at sunrise worked out well," I joke, motioning to the sun that had already started to rise above the trees.

"Yeah, well, some of us couldn't sleep because there was a pack of girls laughing all night," Chris says, giving me a pointed look before breaking out in a big grin. He shifts and moves the pot we had used for cooking. which had been left out on a stump overnight to reveal the top of the stump was fairly dry. He positions himself away from the ring of rain on the edge of one side and takes a seat.

"Hey, don't hate because you weren't in the fun tent," I chide back. I feel Chris's arms circle my waist, and I let out a screech as I'm pulled onto his lap. Giggles erupt from me as I curl up into his chest. I hear a zipper and peek over Chris's shoulder and see Carly and Martha emerge from our tent. Carly's curls are a wild tangle on her head, while Martha has already swept her long dark hair into a clean ponytail with a baseball hat that matches Bill's. "Good morning." Carly yawns as she heads over to the guys' tent to poke her head in.

"Morning," we all say back. Martha smiles at me and Chris, then heads over to stand behind Bill, placing her hands on top of his shoulders. At her touch, he stands and wraps his arms around her, kissing her good morning. Pulling Chris up with me, I head over to untie the food bag from the tree. After it *clunks* back to the ground, we both pull out enough breakfast bars for everyone and start passing them around, handing Carly Fred's bar to give him. "So, when are we going to head out?" Carly asks, taking the bars. "We were talking about that last night, and we aren't sure how bad the trails will be. Maybe we'll leave later this afternoon, after it dries up enough to make the trails passable." We all nod, trying to imagine just how bad the paths probably are.

"Speaking of last night," Fred says, finally emerging from the tent. "What were you girls doing last night?" Taking his breakfast bar from Carly, he unwraps it and eats it all in three bites.

"Oh, we played Mad Libs and it was so much fun!" Carly responds, grabbing Fred's hand and walking over to the rest of us.

They dive deep into a conversation, talking about the game and the stories we created, when Chris comes up behind me and takes my hand.

"Hey, come on let's go." He gives my arm a tug toward the tree line. "Where?" I ask while being towed away. "You'll see."

We walk for a little way until we come up to a clearing with a single tree in the center. It wasn't just any regular tree; it was completely smooth and the trunk was twisted like a tornado, with every branch contorted in odd angles. "Wow," I whisper under my breath. "Yeah, I came across it while we were searching for firewood," Chris says, moving closer to it and giving the trunk a pat. Walking closer, I reach out to one of the curved branches. The wood was soft and smooth from the lack of bark and darker than normal due to the rain.

"This is so cool, Chris. Chris…?" Turning around, I notice Chris is no longer beside me. "Chris?" "Up here."

A hand reaches down from the tree. I look up and see Chris lounging on one of the curves in the branches. I reach up and grasp his hand, trying to navigate my way up the tree. My boot hits a slick spot and I flail. Chris' grip tightens, and he hooks his free hand around the upper part of my left arm. Using his legs to keep him in the tree, he pulls me back up, saving me from falling the four feet from the branch onto my butt. "Careful, Chloe," he warns. "Thanks." I chuckle as I finish the climb to a branch near Chris, settling in the curve beside him. His leg rests against mine, his warmth radiating through our pant legs and helps fight the damp chill the tree is giving off. "This tree is so amazing." I sigh, trying to get the subject off me almost falling. "I wonder what caused this?" I run my hand over the smooth surface, feeling the softness of the wood."Yeah, it is. Could have been a fire caused by lightning, since there's no other close trees that seem to be affected. Or the tree could have just died, and the weather caused it to become partially petrified. Either way, it's just amazing; after all it's been through, it's still so sturdy and strong."

We sit there for a while, pointing out features, like little knolls and differences in the wood that make interesting faces and shapes. It's nice getting away just the two of us, just hanging out and talking.

Chapter Seven

Chloe

We didn't stay in our tree for too long. With a lot of help from Chris, the two of us were able to shimmy down without getting too wet. I grab his hand and we go for a little walk around the clearing. The forest has seemed to come alive while we sat in our tree. The birds are awake now, singing as they flutter from one tree to the next. A squirrel in a nearby pine is scuttling from branch to branch, grabbing pine-cones, and after a quick inspection, tosses them down. The cones make a soft *thud* when they hit the rain-softened ground.

We eventually head back to camp to help the others start packing up. Martha and Carly are just returning from what looks like a walk around the lake as Chris and I emerge from the trees. Chris moves to help Bill break down the tents and pack them back into their bags while I help the others pack up the food and clean up the camp. The tarps are still damp, even after the morning sun has been hitting them, but it can't be helped. We roll them up with the wet side facing in so they won't leak all over the clothes in the bags they are going on. With all of us pitching in, it isn't long before everything is back in bags and the packs are slung back onto shoulders. I let out a small groan of protest and try to roll my shoulders when the weight of the bag settles on me. Shifting the weight around helps a little, and Chris gives me a sly grin.

"Comfy?" he asks, and I roll my eyes in response.

"Everyone got everything?" Fred yells while straightening his bag. He gets a chorus of yeses back, and he moves forward. "Alright, let's get going. We need to reach the second site before dark."

Bill takes the lead again as we all fall in line behind him on the narrow dirt trail.

The path, though muddy, is beautiful. The trees all around us are covered in thick green foliage that glistens from the remaining rain drops. Wildflowers grow freely on either side of the path in shades of blues, reds, purples, and yellows.

Chris occasionally reaches down and picks some of the flowers until he has a small bundle of them. "For you," he says smiling at me. Bending my head down, I take a deep breath in through my nose. It smells amazing, just how summer should smell. "Thank you," I say as I reach for his hand. I pull the flowers back up to my nose, the smell making me smile again.

The path curves in different parts, making it feel like a huge snake looping its body through the trees. The right side of the path gives a nice view into the forest due to the incline of the mountain. But the left side has a sharp drop off, the kind of steep where most people would inch the other way. But even though there are a ton of trees, it does give a nice view of all the neighboring hills. I like to walk a bit closer to that side since sometimes I look down and find a small ridge branching off the mountain, and occasionally, deer are grazing through the trees. On some of the bends you can see where once dry dirt has become so wet from the rain, it has begun to crumble and give way, causing a small mud slide down the hill. Whenever I see that, like the others, I shy away from that side of the path to the other.

We stop for a small water break right after a bend. It's a relief to get the heavy backpack off, even if it's only for a few minutes. The sun is now high enough to see over the trees and the mountain, so we're guessing it's about one o'clock. According to Bill, we still have a couple of hours of hiking left before reaching our next destination

Feeling the beginning of hunger pains in my stomach, I reach into a side pocket of my pack and pull out one of my protein bars. I slowly open it while taking in the view. I take a few bites before offering the rest to Chris, who gratefully takes it and finishes it in about two seconds. I wipe my hands on the front of my pants before bending and begrudgingly heft my pack back on. I try rolling out my shoulders to see if it will rest a bit better. I take a few steps over to the other side of the path and look over. A small stream is running below us, the sound of the water moving over the rocks giving the perfect background noise for a peaceful place to sit and relax. I'm watching a small branch float through the water and around a bend, when to my horror, I feel a hard push against my backpack.

My arms flail as my momentum starts to push me over the edge. My heart is pounding so hard,

I feel like it's about to explode. The once little stream below now seems huge and dangerous. The small trickle I heard before now sounds like it is roaring in my ears. Small bits of rocks get disturbed by my sudden motion and skitter down the hillside in a path my body will surely follow.

Suddenly, the pressure of what was pushing me reverses. Hands grab my backpack and pull me back to safety.

"Saved your life!" a voice yells from behind me. I whip around to see Fred smiling at me. "*WHAT IS WRONG WITH YOU!*" I explode, throwing my hands in the air at him. The flowers Chris gave me, still clutched so tightly in my closed fist a few of the stems started to snap. "*I COULD HAVE DIED!*" "Oh, don't be so dramatic. You wouldn't have. I had you the whole time," he responds with a big grin on his face, acting like he was having the time of his life. I glare at him as he walks away.

"Oh, and by the way…" he says, partially turning around, "you owe me one.""Owe *you* one? You just tried to kill me!"

Totally exasperated, I look over at Chris and fling my arm out at Fred. "I know, I know…" is all he says as he comes over to my side and puts his arm around me. I slip one arm around his waist and let him lead me over to the others as we start for the next curve in the road. I use my free hand to make a crude gesture at Fred's back as he walks away. Smug satisfaction radiates through me when he gets closer to Carly, and she slugs him in the arm and snaps at him to stop being an ass.

"I knew I liked her," I mumble to Chris.

Chapter Eight

Chloe

About forty minutes after the whole Fred incident, we finally hit a trail marker that, according to Bill means we are right on time, and in a couple of hours, we would be all set up at our final camping spot, though I never saw such a marker. We had seen a few other people on the trail, both passing us on the way up because there are fewer of them and coming back down. A few impressed me with just how much gear they had with them. It made my little backpack from the local outdoor co-op feel insufficient.

The one good thing about the rain on the trail is that it makes animal tracks a lot more defined and noticeable. I'm following a trail of deer tracks on the side of the path when I notice my boot lace trailing on the ground. I slowly readjust my pack so I can bend over and retie my shoe. "What's wrong?" Chris asks, turning around. "Oh, my boot just came untied. Go on, I'll catch up." I wave for him to keep going as the others haven't noticed my stop.

"Okay…" he says a bit hesitantly. "I'll run up to them and let them know to hold on."

"Sounds good." I flash him a smile and watch as he rounds the corner before bending my head to pay attention to what I'm doing.

As I start rolling my pant leg up and out of the way and grab my now muddy shoelaces, I hear something approach from behind me. I stand, ignoring my shoe, and see two people on big mountain bikes quickly coming up the trail. They are closely hugging the inside of the path to avoid any of the loose, unpredictable trail edges. I'm hesitant to move to that side, but to avoid getting run over, I scoot over to the edge of the trail to give them as much room as possible. The path is a lot narrower up here since we were closer to the peak than it was where we started at the base. The first bike passes by without an issue, and he even offers a small wave of thanks. But as the second comes closer, the more of the trail he seems to take. I can tell he's a lot more uncomfortable with the terrain than his friend. His eyes are so focused on the path in front of his wheel that I doubt he even knows someone else is here. When he passes by dangerously close to me, I instinctively take a small jump back to avoid a handle bar hitting me in the chest. The earth my feet landed on is soft and crumbly from the rain and quickly gives way under my weight. I have a horrible sensation of weightlessness right before I'm falling.

Chapter Nine

Chris

"How long does it take to tie a shoe?" Carly whines. She has already taken her pack off and is using it as a chair. "Yeah. Chris, go see what's taking he so long," Bill seconds. "Alright." I sigh, pushing myself off the tree I was leaning against. I had been wondering what was taking so long but I didn't want to go back and rush her. Chloe is not a person who likes to be hurried.

"Hey, Chloe, everyone is getting restless." I pause. Chloe isn't on the trail where I had left her. "Chloe?" I call out a little louder but get no response. Scratching the back of my head, I walk until I'm around the next curve in the path, thinking she must have dropped something and had gone back looking for it. "Chloe!" Again, no response. I make a small circuit through the trees off the side of the trail in case she had needed to make a bathroom stop and had somehow gotten lost. There is no sign of anything in the trees, and no footprints or disruptions in the dirt, leaving zero sign of her. I feel panic work its way into my gut. *Something isn't right. Where is she?*

I quickly jog back to the others when I notice flowers scattered near the edge of the path right before it begins to curve. How had I missed that before? Carefully, I pick some of them up. Underneath are the distinct marks of tire tread from one of the bikes that had passed us a little bit ago. Those guys had no business being up here. Not only was it not allowed this high up but after the rain we had last night, only a fool would ride on this trail. Getting closer to the end of the path I notice the edge has been upset by something and has started caving away.

I suddenly feel like I am in a movie, the cliche 'this can't be happening' playing on a loop in my head. Slowly, I reach the edge, and I am expecting to find Chloe laying down at the bottom of the cliff, dead and broken. To my relief, I see no such thing. The hill angles to an extreme degree and a small ledge protruding from the cliff edge obscures my view the rest of the way down. Plants and rocks have been upturned the whole way down obvious signs of something going down fast. Cupping my hands around my mouth, I yell her name as loud as I can. Pausing for a second, I strain to try to make out any kind of response. I'm on my third try, leaning slightly forward to project my voice farther when my feet start to slip out from underneath me. Quickly, I throw my weight backward, landing on my butt on solid, damp ground. I can hear a few rocks tumble down. I can see it now, how she fell. The dirt is soft and still crumbling from where I just was a few moments ago. It wouldn't have taken much if she wasn't paying attention for it to give way before she had the chance to move.

Frantically, I search for a way to get down there, to get to her. There is no clear game trail or anything I can try to grab onto to help me descend slowly and safely.

"Chris, dude, what's wrong?" a voice asks from behind me.

Turning, I see the others hurrying around the corner, and I run over to them, panting. "Chloe... I think... she fell... over the side." I point over to the edge. "But I can't find a way down; it's too steep. Maybe if I can make it to the ledge down there, I might be able to see her."

The guys gingerly make their way over top the ledge and look over. "There's no way, man," Fred says, rubbing the back of his head. Martha and Carly slowly move closer. Martha's face is full of worry as she takes in the scene below. Carly has tears welling up in her eyes as she clutches Fred's arm, keeping him from moving too close to the edge.

"That ledge is barely stable as it is. If it couldn't hold Chloe's weight, then there's no way it's going to hold any of ours." Bill comes up and puts his hand on my shoulder. "Don't worry, Chris; if she's down there, we will find her. Fred, pull out the satellite phone and call this in. If you can't get a signal, keep hiking up till you do. Girls, find all the rope and emergency gear you can and put it in a pile." I walk back over to the edge, my heart racing. I'm grateful for their help; I know they will keep their cool and get everything into motion for me. I crouch, trying to get a better look through the trees. The path of destruction she made is more prominent at the top. Now that I'm taking a longer look, I can see a large section of the ledge had broken off recently, with plants half uprooted and overturned rocks. The farther I look down, the more the trail starts to fade. "Don't worry, Chloe," I murmur. "I will find you."

Chapter Ten

Chloe

Everything hurts. I don't think there's a single part of me that isn't scraped, scratched, bruised, or broken. I try to open my eyes, but my vision is still dark and cloudy. There is a slight ringing in my ears and a pounding in my head, slow and continuous, never giving me any relief. The rest of my body feels worse though, and I know there will be bruises everywhere and possibly some broken bones. Every sensation is coming back to me all at once, making every injury feel so connected, I can't tell where one stops and another begins. I keep opening and closing my eyes, and as I do, the darkness in my vision slowly starts to fade. I keep blinking and things are starting to finally come into focus, but the scene in front of me is confusing. I had expected to see the sky when I opened my eyes. But it is still dark, just a different kind than before. As my view comes into focus, I feel clumps of dirt and dry leaves tickling my nose. I'm lying on my stomach, and I try to wiggle my fingers, and thankfully, that motion doesn't hurt too much. I slowly start pulling my arms underneath my body to brace against them. Twigs crack under the weight of my hands, and I can feel dead leaves crinkle against my skin. With a loud groan I push off the damp ground and roll over onto my back. As soon as my face leaves the ground, I am momentarily blinded by the brightness of the sun. My vision darkens slightly, again and the world spins from the sudden surge of movement, but after a few blinks, I'm able to see the outlines of the trees above me. Small dots still dance across my vision, and I feel something hot and wet on my face. I wipe at it with the back of my hand and it comes back bloody. "Fantastic," I huff out, laying my arm back out to my side. I lay there, looking at the sky as I try to remember what happened.

The memories slowly start trickling back; the bikes, the ground falling away, the feeling of panic so fierce, it makes my stomach knot. I remember the sharp pain of the first impact knocking the wind out of me as I hit the rocks below, but my momentum didn't stop there. Another image flashes, my hands clawing at the ground as I keep rolling, not being able to get a hold of anything solid as I upturn everything I pass. Rocks tumble with me until, on one rotation, my head slams into something, followed by a flash of blinding pain, and that's when everything goes dark.

The memory has me reaching my hand back to the side of my head. I wince and suck in a rattling breath when my fingers brush over a large knot that seems to have a steady stream of blood coming from it. I also find a lot of sticks and leaves tangled in the mess on top of my head. I lower my hand and roll my head from side to side, taking a look at my surroundings. I find the hillside I must have tumbled down. Dirt and rocks were turned loose, and a couple of bushes had been smashed flat and in pieces. You can definitely tell something had come down hard and fast, causing unrestrained chaos with it. I'm trying to see everything in my line of sight without sitting up yet, when in the corner of my vision, my left leg catches my attention. The blood and dirt caked on my torn pant leg isn't what is so alarming… it's the impossible angle it's cocked at that makes my stomach drop in panic. As if seeing it reminds my brain that this and other injuries exist, the first wave a pain rolls over my entire body. It is sudden and blinding, and I try biting back the scream, but the high-pitch breaks through. Whatever had been blocking the pain before is definitely gone now. Wave after wave of pain rolls through me causing my hands to curl in the wet dirt at my sides. The leg seems to trigger all the nerves in my body at once, allowing me to feel every hurt the fall had caused. My head is pounding, the skin on my hands is raw and sore from trying to slow my descent. A sharp pain jabs at my ribs with every inhale, but the worst is my leg. I have never so much as broken a finger before, so this feeling is something I have never experienced.

When the pain finally becomes somewhat manageable, I take a chance to look at my other leg; thankfully, it appears in one piece as my arms are as well.

Slowly, I pull myself into a sitting position, careful not to move my injured leg, and my vision blurs yet again, as the pounding in my head becomes almost audible as blood rushes to my brain. My muscles ache from the fall, but at the moment, it is all fairly tolerable compared to my leg. I don't want to risk looking down at my leg again, so I decide to do a thorough inspection on my arms instead. There are several cuts in my shirt, revealing matching scratches on the skin underneath, and I'm completely caked in mud and random bits of foliage. Rolling up the sleeves of my shirt, I find a nasty bruise is forming on one of my elbows, the skin already turning into a blotchy mix of blue and purple, but other than that, my upper extremities look fine for the most part. I slowly allow my eyes to travel lower. My stomach and sides look relatively unharmed, and the sharp pain from earlier may just be bruised ribs and not broken, as I had feared. I lift the edge of my shirt to check the skin below. A large bruise is also forming on my right side. With trembling fingers, I gently probe at the purple skin. It's definitely tender, but there is no sharp pain indicating the ribs are broken underneath, just a dull throb, and I let out a sigh of relief. Next, I recheck my right leg, that looks uninjured, still avoiding looking to my left. I gingerly bring my knee up and stretch it out again. Like everything else, my muscles are definitely sore but thankfully, it should be able to bear weight.

I suck in a deep breath and brace myself as I let my gaze drift back to the injured leg. I can feel my body start to tremble as I notice more and more details of the injury. The pant leg is still in one piece, aside from a large gash just above the knee, which makes the sight horrible to look at. The khaki material is blotched with blood stains, and true to form, completely covered in dirt. I do feel a sense of relief that I was able to keep both shoes on my feet through the fall, the one still untied from before. I attempt to wiggle my foot, more out of shocked curiosity and the small thread of hope that it isn't really as bad as it looks. But as soon as the muscles in my thighs try to pull on the ones in my shin, a sharp searing pain rips through right at the point where my leg takes its unnatural bend, but below that, nothing. I'm not quite sure if I really can't feel my foot or if the pain in my leg is just so intense that it drowns out all other feeling. A strong urge makes me want to roll up the pant leg and see just how bad the break is. But I know there is also a risk that truly seeing the full extent at this time could send me completely into shock, and that wouldn't help anything.

Prying my eyes from my body, I survey the area around me. The cliff I had used for my impromptu descent looks as if it could have been a wall made out of nature. The angle of its incline is so sharp, there's no way I could hike back up there, even before I was hurt. Yet again, the realization that I even survived the fall at all truly astounds me. Glancing around the small clearing I am sitting in, it appears that it is actually the bottom of a draw, with steep hills completely surrounding me. I twist my head around, trying to see if there is a break in the endless hills. A feeling of complete and total helplessness takes over me. My shoulders slump forward, and I feel hot tears pool in my eyes, stinging as they run down my cheeks. I use the back of my hand to wipe them away, but more just follow. Soon, sobs wrack through my chest and out of my mouth. I fling my hands down into the mud and just let the cry happen.

What am I supposed to do now? How on earth am I supposed to get out of here? Do they even know I'm gone? My sobbing slowly stops at that thought. Of course, Chris would know I'm missing. I'm sure he's trying to find me right now.

"Come on, Chloe," I whisper to myself, trying to find a clean piece of my shirt to wipe my face. "Enough of your pity party." I look at the hills again. One doesn't seem quite as steep as the others; it has a little bit of a slope to it, but a small enough one that I may be able to get onto, and there is what looks like an old game trail winding around the brush.

"Alright," I mumble to myself as I gather my strength. "Time to find a way out of here." I glance near my immediate surroundings and there is a large branch, similar to the one Chris had turned into a walking stick for me yesterday, within arm's reach. I quickly look around for my backpack, but another memory flashes in my mind of it being ripped off during the fall. I am hopeful that it might have followed me to the bottom. I can't see it anywhere, so it must have gotten caught up on something up high, so I settle for just grabbing the stick. I slowly lean a little bit to grab the stick, but just the small movement has me gasping and grunting as the bruised skin of my sides stretch. I grasp out and snag the branch, relaxing slightly as I pull it into my lap. It's not as smooth as the one Chris had made for me, and it has several small sticks poking out of the body. I slowly started bending and twisting those to try to create an easier piece to hold onto. I grab the whole branch with both hands and carefully bend it. It gives slightly, but it seems to be a pretty hardy piece and should be able to support my body weight. Jamming it into the ground with both hands, I slowly bring my good leg underneath me and use both it and the stick to haul myself up.

As soon as the bad leg starts to get pulled up and straighten pain flares through me so strong, I am afraid for a second that I will lose conciseness again. For a moment, I think I will lose my grip on the one thing that is keeping me upright. My knuckles turn white as I tighten my sweat-slickened grip, and a scream escapes my lips as I continued to pull myself into a standing position.

Once I am standing semi-straight, I can feel the weight of the bum leg as it limply hangs underneath me. I position my walking stick on my right side, leaning as much weight as I can onto it. Doing so raises my left leg enough that the toe of my boot lifts off the ground. Using both hands, I walk the stick forward and tentatively use the momentum to bring my right foot forward. I do this again and again around my small clearing, finding the branch definitely supports my weight just fine. My left leg pulses every time it swings with the momentum, but the pain is manageable as long as I make sure the toe of my foot doesn't catch on any of the taller rocks or branches. As soon as I'm confident in my makeshift crutch, I turn to the ridge I had seen earlier and start my climb out of my hell-hole.

Chapter Eleven

Chris

"Okay everyone," Chief Wallace bellows into the megaphone, his outline lit up in the fading sky from the lights of the ambulances. "You all should have a copy of the photo we passed around earlier. We are looking for Chloe Whiteshed, twenty-two-year-old female, five foot six, with blonde hair and blue eyes. Most likely injured. If you find her or any signs of her, radio in on channel three. Remember, stay in your groups and pay attention to your surroundings; we don't need any more accidents." He gazes around at the crowd. "Alright, let's go."

I watch as the people around me start to hike up the mountain in groups. Some I recognize from school, while others I remember from around town, and some are other hikers from out of the area who had noticed the commotion and volunteered to help. Every group is equipped with basic search and rescue supplies outfitted by either the sheriff's department, the park rangers, or from gear they already had in their cars.

Watching all the people hike up the hill has me remembering the hours after Chloe's fall. When we couldn't find a safe way down the edge of the hillside, we all ran down the path until we had found another group camped down the way with bikes. After explaining the situation, the group lent some of us their bikes so we could get down faster. After a few hours, we had met up with the emergency vehicles at the highest point where the vehicles could go on their service roads just below the camp ground at the pond. After that point, park rangers and game wardens usually used horses or four-wheelers to get to emergency situations. Thank God, Fred had been able to get a signal with the satellite phone and had called everything that had happened into the station. After surveying the area, the emergency response team sent by the nearest ranger station came to the decision it would be safer to try to get to Chloe by walking up from the bottom of the mountain. Trying to scale down the way she went was risky and apparently, that hillside branched into several different draws she could have gone down. After many more phone calls, we had almost every police officer and emergency responder from every small town along the highway surrounding us all here to help search within a few hours. We were also able to get the word out enough that a small group of townspeople had gathered to aid in the search. Chloe's mother had arrived with the chief in near hysterics, with Ethan and Lilly sitting right next to her.

Explaining to Mrs. Whiteshed that I had no idea where Chloe was and that I had not been with her, so I wasn't one hundred percent sure what had happened, had been one of the hardest things I had ever done. The despair on her face nearly ripped me in half. She had grasped my hand and squeezed tightly, trying to be reassuring. But even if she didn't blame me, I blamed myself. Releasing my hand, she had turned and put her arm around Ethan and led him and his baby sister toward the makeshift basecamp the police had set up.

Turning, I head over to where my group is waiting, which consists of Bill, Fred, Martha, and Tom. I don't know Tom well, but I know Chloe does, so when he had come up and asked to join our group, I nodded in thanks. Carly volunteered to stay behind with Lilly so Chloe's mom and brother could join the search.

I look up in the sky; another rain-storm is making its way in slowly.

"Ready guys?" No one really answers, but instead we all just turn and start toward the tree line. I take the lead, taking long strides, trying to get into the trees quickly. Slowly, I look down at the picture in my hands. It is a picture I had taken last summer when Chloe and I went to the amusement park up north. We had gone to the picnic area for lunch, and she was sitting on a blanket we had packed, smiling. It's the picture I carry in my wallet, and when the police asked Mrs. Whiteshed for a description, I pulled this out for them instead. They quickly had it passed around the volunteers who had showed up first. They then had each search party group leader take a picture of the photo with their phones so they could all have a copy as a reference. This proved to be the quickest way to get it to everyone without the need for cell service, which up here, was spotty at best and with another storm rolling in, who knows when we'd have it. Chief Wallace sent a deputy down the mountain until he got service so that a copy of the photo could be emailed to the hospital too, just in case she got there on her own or if someone else already on the mountain came across her and brought her in.

As if another girl would be wandering the woods by herself.

"I'll find you, Chloe, I promise," I whisper to the picture before tucking it into my inside jacket pocket.

. . . .

"Can everyone see now?" I ask, adjusting the headlight. "Yeah, that's much better," one of them murmurs. Another light comes on, and then another, until the group is standing in a little circle of light. We all are exhausted, but none of us are willing to head back. Even though it is getting dark, the fear that we might miss her keeps us all on our toes. Our streams of light separate as the group starts to move again, the leaves and sticks crunching under my feet. An owl hoots and sweeps over our heads when Fred's light disturbs him on his branch. A loud *thud* sends all our lights spinning, only to find Martha on the ground with her foot wedged in between a fallen tree and one of its branches.

"Come on," Bill groans as he hoists Martha back to her feet. "Sorry. I'm good," she huffs as she wipes the soft dirt off her hands and knees. "Maybe we should head back and rest for a little bit, then we can try another path?" Bill offers. "It won't do anyone any good if we end up breaking ankles trying to navigate this terrain in the dark.""No. We have to keep looking." Shining my light back forward, I start hiking through some more brush. I can vaguely hear the others follow behind me.

Chapter Twelve

Chloe

The ridge is a lot harder to get up than I had originally thought. Hiking up a hill while using a stick to replace the leg you're dragging behind makes for very slow-going progress. Every gopher hole, soft spot, and loose rock has me stumbling and off-balanced. And even more unfortunate for me, the surrounding mountain and trees have made the sun disappear a little quicker now that I am so far down into the bottom. That, plus the pain in my leg, makes it easy to decide to stop and find a place to spend the night. The air gets a chill to it when the sky grows dim. I can also feel blood running down my pant leg again from the gash above my knee. I hadn't noticed it before, but it is now completely soaking my pants, turning them a dark reddish-black color with mud caked everywhere. Grinding my teeth and taking deep breaths in and out of my nose, I move a couple of more hops before finding a mound of earth to lean against. Slowly, I ease myself down, trying to move the leg as little as possible. Once I'm settled, I slowly roll up my pant leg, and a small shriek escapes my lips as I pass the break. The skin surrounding the break is black and blue and slightly sunken in, but I try not to focus too much on that at the moment. I don't stop rolling the pant leg until I can see the cut. It's definitely not pretty; the wound is about three inches long and deep enough where I can see thick muscle. It's bleeding steadily, running off in different directions down my leg. I chance another glance down at the break; the angle at which it is sticking out makes me want to throw up, but at least bone hasn't broken through. I suck in a few deep breaths and try to calm my stomach as it twists and churns at the sight of my mangled leg.

I bury my face in my hands, and I run my fingers over my matted hair. Grateful for a small distraction, I start picking some debris out of the tangled mess and finger-brush through some of the smaller tangles. My head is still pounding from earlier, and with all the extra exertion, just looking straight is becoming increasingly hard. Tears slowly start trailing down my cheeks again. Why hasn't anyone found me yet? The dark questions flip through my thoughts again as I sit in the darkening forest. *Where are they? Do they even know I'm gone? Of course, they do; I have to quit thinking like this.* But I can't seem to help it. The longer I'm down here, the grimmer my thoughts become.

"Come on, Chloe," I shake myself. "Stop crying and get yourself off this mountain." There is nothing I can think of to help my leg, so I carefully roll the pant leg back down. Grabbing the stick again, I hoist myself back up and start hopping toward the trees, looking for shelter before it gets completely dark.

. . . .

Falling to my knees again, I suck in a deep breath and look up. All care of my injured leg is gone. I'm so exhausted, I can barely even feel it at this point. Strings of hair fall into my face, and all I see are miles of terrain that's at an ungodly angle. I slump my head back down, trying to catch my breath. "Come on, Chloe," I grit. "One, two… three." I lift myself back onto my feet. I look up and see a small outcropping about fifty yards ahead of me, which I mark as my next resting spot. That's how I have been able to keep going. I try to focus on a small landmark ahead of me and tell myself that I just have to make it that far before I can rest again. Each time I reach the new spot, I take a moment to catch my breath, then search for a new landmark just ahead of me. All the while, I am also searching for an adequate place to rest for the night. Slowly, I start side-hilling, trying to get to the crest of the hill so it will be easier to go up.

The sun sank down below the trees about an hour ago, and the forest has begun to get darker, making it difficult to make out trees that are just a few feet in front of me.

Finally, I reach my next goal, taking a pause I look down the side I had just climbed. In reality, it wasn't that far, but it took me roughly a half an hour to go up something that would have normally taken me minutes. My head becomes dizzy again. My vision begins to sway, making the trees look like they're dancing. I lean onto my crutch more and more until I start to slide, sending rocks tumbling down to the tree line. Luckily, my stick anchors me and keeps me from losing what little ground I have covered. I slowly sink into a sitting position and look around again.

Unfortunately, the ridge I am now sitting on is open, with nothing but rocks, and therefore, no options for shelter. The only cover I can see right now, even in the dark, are the trees themselves. My stomach sinks at the fact that the only option now is to go down the other side.

Feeling defeated, I lay back with a groan and look up at the sky. Although it is dark and stormy, I can see a few stars poking their way around some rain clouds. The gray, billowy forms break up the solid darkness of the sky. All I want to do is lay here on these rocks and go to sleep, but I know I'm no match for the elements. *I really need shelter.*

After a few more minutes of rest, I begrudgingly make my way to the other side of the hill. The promise of shelter is the only thing tempting enough to give up that last bit of ground I had just covered.

The walk down the little ridge is a lot easier than the way up. In certain smooth places, I sit and kind of slide my way down. One thing I begin to notice though, is the blood trail I am leaving behind. It is faint, especially in the dim lighting, but small drops of dark red speckle the rocks behind me. I had tried wrapping a shred of my shirt around the cut on my leg during one of my breaks, but it has done little to staunch the bleeding.

I reach the tree line right when the rain starts to fall. It is dryer under the canopy of trees, but water still filters through the leaves and pine needles. I can feel it tapping my hair, and my shoulders are slowly getting damp through my shirt. Eventually, after wandering long enough that my shirt is now almost completely soaked through, I find a little area where branches from several trees have grown together, forming a small den. The inside is dry, and the wall of branches keeps it fairly warm compared to the outside. Damp and cold, I crawl inside and decide to look at my leg again. The bleeding has finally stopped, but the cut is filthy. Even in the dark, I can see it's packed with mud and who knows what else, and more than likely, it is going to get infected. The skin around the broken bone is looking even worse. The dim lighting causes the already dark bruises to look absolutely dreadful, giving a stark contrast to my white skin. I reach over to the wall of branches and slowly break a few of the longer and straighter ones off so I can make a splint. I rip off the bottom half of my hiking pants, then tear it into strips. Even though they are bloody and caked with mud, they are all I have. I slowly press the straightest stick against my broken leg. I don't even try to hold back the scream, and I don't stop until I have tied the splint securely to my leg. I lay back against the layer of old pine needles scattered on the ground utterly exhausted. I stare at the branches overhead, praying that I might fall asleep soon.

Chapter Thirteen

Chloe

Miraculously, I either fell asleep or passed out from the throbbing in my head and leg. But either way, I don't know exactly how long I have been asleep, maybe only a couple of hours since it is still dark out when I am woken up by a noise outside my little den. It is still raining steadily; the rain drops thudding softly on my makeshift roof. Thankfully, it did its job, and I am still dry. Drowsily, I look around, wondering what caused me to wake up. The pounding in my head has decreased slightly, and the pain in my leg is no worse than it had been before I fell asleep. I am just beginning to wonder if I had bumped my leg with the other when, somewhere outside, behind my den wall, a twig snaps. My breath catches and I strain my ears to pick up another noise. I'm wondering if it may have just been a one-off, but then I hear the sharp snap of branches breaking. Slowly, I sit up and look out the entry-way, but inky blackness shrouds the forest, making it nearly impossible to even see my hand in front of me. With my lack of fire, or one of the several flashlights from my backpack, it is impossible to see anything through the darkness. Another branch snaps, and my heart stutters. *Is it my imagination or did that one sound closer to the front of my little hiding spot?* I quickly scoot myself to the back of the den using my good leg. Branches poke into my back as I try not to move around too much or make any noise. The last thing I want to do is make one of the many branches surrounding me snap and alert whatever is outside that I am here, just as it had done. A thought enters my head, and it suddenly strikes me that it might be a person, maybe someone I know is looking for me. "Hello?" I holler. I only hear silence and rain, and even the stick cracking has stopped.

"Hello? I'm over here!" I yell even louder. I crawl back through the dry bed I had been asleep on moments before and poke my head out of the opening of the den. There are no reflections from flashlights or lanterns on the trees or in the falling rain. I see no movement and a chill runs down my spine, and I get the eerie feeling that I am being watched by something in the darkness. Remembering the sign about the wildlife out here, I pull my head back into the den. I sit with my arms wrapped around my good leg, shivering from cold and fear, and I don't think I even so much as blinked. Every little noise makes me whip my head around blindly as I sit here, waiting.

Chapter Fourteen

Chris

It was sheer determination that kept the group moving. We are all completely exhausted from hiking and the lack of sleep, but no one complained, not even when the rain started. The storm made everything more frustrating; knowing that any evidence of her trail could be disappearing right now.

We bumped into other search parties several times, and we shared where we had been and if there was any sign of her. The conversations never lasted long before we split off again. We met up with Chloe's mother and brother's group, and it was a sad sight like everyone else they were soaked from the rain, their boots and pants caked with mud. Their faces looked how I felt mine must have looked depressed, sad, and scared but Mrs.

Whiteshed had a look of hope in her eyes. She held a look of sheer determination, like Chloe would step out from behind a tree any second.

The moment she saw me, she locked her eyes on mine and marched right up to me. *This is it.* She hadn't snapped at me yet, like I thought she would have when she first showed up, but I had been waiting for it, waiting for her to put all the blame on me for her daughter being lost in the woods. And I deserved it; I was already blaming myself, so why shouldn't she? I was supposed to look after her. I was the one who was supposed to keep Chloe safe, and I had failed.

When she finally stands in front of me, her actions catch me off guard. Instead of slapping me or screaming, she throws her arms around me and hugs me to her. I instantly wrap my arms around her and hug her back. She is what I wish my mother had always been, kind, nurturing, loving. "I will find her, I promise," I whisper to her, hugging her tighter. "I know you will," she whispers, squeezing me once more before drawing back. She slowly goes back to her group, putting one arm around Ethan and slowly leads him east with the rest of them. Ethan looks back at me once, his face reflecting in the light of their flashlights.

A memory strikes me from a few years ago, at their father's funeral. I remember comforting Chloe through that whole time. I was at their house every day, and right now, Ethan's face looks the same as the day of the funeral. He looks sad and hopeless, like a scared little kid who just lost a very important person in their life.

I stand there, frozen by his expression, even after he turns back around and his mother guides him down the path. I suddenly realize I have to find her and bring her back, not just for me, but for her little brother and sister, too. What would this do to them, to lose another family member? I square my shoulders and turn back to where my group is spread out, searching.

We continue to hike, moving higher every few minutes. "She has got to be here," I say. "She couldn't have got far, and this is the side she went down, right?" "Yeah," Fred answers. "This is it, but it's so dark, we can't see anything, and the rain is washing away any track she may have left."

While the rain has finally let up some, it has down poured long enough to wipe even our tracks from the muddy trail.

"And there's so many fingers that come off each side and lead in different directions… If she's moving, she could have crossed over into any of those and become more lost," Bill adds, flashing his light around for emphasis. And he's right. Chloe is strong-willed, and even if she was hurt, she would try to find a way to get herself out. And she could have easily gotten turned around and lost given the area.

But there is only so far she could have gone before it got dark, and then she would have tried to find cover.

We are all standing still, sweeping the dark around us with our headlamps, when a series of cracks makes us all halt. "Whoa…" Bill whispers. "What was that?"

Our heads started turning in search of the noise. Whatever made the noise is definitely not human; we have been hearing humans walk all over the forest floor all night, and what we just heard was a distinctly different sound. Suddenly, I catch sight of the tail of a raccoon disappear into some bushes. "It's just a raccoon," I yell. "Nothing to worry about." "Yeah," Tom's voice rings out. "But it's a good reminder that we are not alone out here." I nod as an eerie feeling washes over the group, and I watch the other headlamps slowly sweep over the forest again.

"Just stay close together and we will be fine. Nothing will try to get us when we are in a group this big." We start searching again, not venturing out quite as far apart as before but feeling safer. A small voice in my head whispers, "But what about Chloe? She's all alone…" Squaring my shoulders, I march on. *Nothing will happen to Chloe.*

Chapter Fifteen

Chloe

Several times, I swear I hear heavy footfalls around my small camp during the night. A part of me wants to yell out again, but I'm not making that mistake again. I don't want to risk drawing the attention of something else looking for a dry place for the night.

At some point, the rain stops, but I don't notice until the sun starts to rise. Cramped and stiff, I slowly work myself out of the curled-up ball I had been in all night. I stretch as much as I can without hurting myself and look around. My mouth feels like sandpaper, and my stomach is beyond the growling stage of hunger and is now feeling like it is gnawing at my insides. I spot some leaves attached to a small tree growing at the front of my makeshift camp, and the leaves are curled inward, creating a small bowl. Looking closer, I see they captured some of the rain-water. Carefully, I tip them one at a time into my mouth and let the cool water trickle down my throat. It's not a lot, but my tongue no longer feels rough and my throat feels slightly better.

Finally, I feel like I am able to concentrate a little more, and I take a closer look at my surroundings now that it's light out. The ground is still angled, but the trees are packed closer together than they were higher up. Nothing looks familiar at all. Looking down at my hands, I notice some of my fingernails have ripped and are caked with dried blood and dirt. The backs of my hands are also dirty and smudged, and small cuts criss-cross across the skin. I look around and spot a small rock patch that seems to have also collected some of the rain from last night. I inch myself over carefully and slowly press one of my hands into the small puddle of water. The cold water swirls over the back of my hand, causing the small cuts on my skin to sting. Slowly, some of the filth on my skin starts to wash away, staining the puddle a murky gray-brown. I switch hands, placing my other one in the water. This one takes a little more scrubbing to get clean, probably because the water is now so dirty. By the time I take the second hand out, the water is dark brown with a slight film swirling on the surface. The cold air bites at my damp hands, and I try my best to tuck them under my arms to protect them while they dry. My stomach growls so loudly, I think the birds fluttering from a nearby tree can hear it.

I try to wrack my brain to remember any foraging tips I had read in one of the guide books I had purchased when we first decided to do this hiking trip. Chris made fun of me when I had picked it up off the shelf at the outdoor supply store, but I told him it was just as important as the boots and packs we were there to purchase.

"You're from here; why do you need a guide book?" Chris had asked after grabbing the book from my hand to read the back cover.

"Because," I countered, snatching it back, "last time I checked, neither of us are outdoorsmen. What happens if we get stuck? Or lost?"

"We are not going to get lost. Bill's done this hike before." He sighed but said no more as I stacked the book on top of my hiking boots box and walked up to the check-out counter.

I smile at the memory. I remember flipping through the book and after reading the 'What to Pack' chapter, I had focused on the 'How to Properly Break in Your Boots' chapter, but I had only skimmed through the 'Edible Plants' chapter. And if I am being honest, I mostly looked at the colorful, detailed pictures. I'm kicking myself because I hadn't taken the time to focus on the descriptions written underneath the pictures.

I glance around at some of the foliage around me, hoping that something will strike a memory of one of the pictures. A few small plants look familiar, but nothing I am definite on enough to risk putting into my mouth. I limp forward to try to get a better look beyond the first layer of growth, and a tall, leafy plant grabs my attention. Moving closer, I instantly recognize it. Anyone who grows up around the forests all learn that this is one plant you want to avoid, unless you want painful hives to pop up on your skin. I gently grab the tip of one of the leaves and lift it to expose the plant stock. Sure enough, small hair-like thorns cover the plant, *stinging nettle*. I instantly get excited because I do recognize this plant from the book. I remember because of how odd I found it to be in the edible plant section. One would think that something called stinging nettle shouldn't be put anywhere close to your mouth, but this plant is one hundred percent edible. I remember from what I had read that you are to soak the leaves in water to remove the stinging toxin. After that, the leaves are okay for consumption. The book also noted that many people describe the flavor as being a cross between spinach and cucumber.

Carefully, I start pulling the leafy parts of the plant from the stalk and shove them into one of my cargo pockets. As I reach around the plant to pull a piece from the opposite side, my hand brushes too close to the body of the pant. A rather large needle pierces the skin and breaks off the plant.

"Shit!" I yell out, pulling my hand to my chest. I firmly, yet carefully, grasp the needle and pull it from my hand, careful to make sure none of it breaks off and stays buried under the skin where I have no hope of getting it out. A sharp stinging sensation spreads through the area around the small puncture hole left on my hand. I quickly rub the area with my other hand, hoping the sensation will fade quickly.

I look up and glare at the plant. "Stupid plant," I mutter and look back down at my hand. The skin is red, and small hives have already began to pop up. The stinging sensation is slowly fading, replaced with a less painful but more annoying itching. I try my hardest to ignore the irritation as I carefully extract a few more leaves from the plant.

Once I have filled both my side pockets and secured the little snap to close them, I slowly start making my way back to my little tree fort. Luckily, since there was so much rain last night, there are plenty of puddles to choose from to soak the leaves in. I hobble over to a grouping of some larger puddles and pull out the slightly crumpled leaves from my pockets. I gently submerge them in the puddles, and the movement stirs some of the mud that has settled on the bottom. Once my pockets are empty and the puddles are full of dark leaves, I sit back and stare at them. The book hadn't mentioned how long to soak them for... Is it more of a rinse or an overnight soak? As I sit and debate when to pull them out, I notice the puddle containing the leaves is getting a slightly orange tint to it, different from the dark brown dirt that had swirled around in it earlier. Carefully, I scoop the leaves out of the puddle. The orange water runs down the leaves and makes a small orange stream down my hand, dripping back into the small pool of water below. Curious, I move to the next largest puddle and slowly set the leaves into it and sit back, watching intently. Slowly, the water in this puddle also gets a slightly orange tint to it, although less concentrated than the first one. Excitedly, I repeat this process until I pull them

from the final puddle, and the water shows no hint
of the coppery color. I give them a gentle shake
to remove the excess water from the leafy mass in
my hands.

A dark shadow slowly moves over me, blocking
the sunshine from filtering down through the
trees around me. I glance up and see another
round of rain clouds forming in the sky above me.
A rain-drop falls onto my cheek, and I quickly
tuck the leaves into my pocket, causing a cool
dampness to press through my pants to my skin.
I grab my walking stick and move as quickly as
I can manage back to my tree house. I nestle
down on the dry pine needles just as the rain starts
to fall in full force again. I pull the leaves out
and hesitantly put one in my mouth and chew.
Thankfully, there is no stinging like there had
been on my hand, and an earthy flavor similar
to how the book had described fills my mouth.
My stomach twists at the promise of food, and
it takes every ounce of self-control not to shove
the small handful of leaves I had harvested into
my mouth at once. I resist, knowing that all
that would do is probably make me sick. I make
myself eat the leaves slowly, one at a time, savoring
the feeling of having food in my mouth again.
Too quickly, my hands are empty and so are my

pockets. I carefully shift myself into a somewhat comfortable position and try to wait out the rain. My stomach gurgles as it digests the first food I have eaten since the breakfast bar I had… Was it only yesterday morning?

Between the comfort of finding food and the gentle sound of the rain falling through the trees and softly *thumping* onto the forest floor, I soon find myself nodding off. The storm clouds darken the forest around me, simulating dusk, and I close my eyes and slowly let myself drift off to sleep.

Chapter Sixteen

Chloe

The rain has slowed to a drizzle when I wake from my early morning nap. My stomach rumbles; the small snack of leaves I had eaten earlier must have already worked their way through my system. I pull myself out of my den and glance around. I quickly decide that the best thing to do now is to take advantage of the break in the rain and look for a path to make my way off this mountain.

I look around again, trying to decide what direction to go in next. I tried uphill yesterday, so I guess I could try downhill today. Now that I am out of that ravine, multiple paths are available to try. One on my left seems to have more animal tracks walking down it than the others, and I am hopeful it eventually hits a road or one of those small mountain farms we had seen on the way up. But either way, it's sure as hell going to be easier than going uphill. The downside is, I don't know the terrain. I could just as easily walk myself right into an area like the one I fell into, or a dead end where the only option would be to turn around and hike backup hill again.

Going uphill, I had some hope of coming across the trails my friends and I had used. But at this point, I am so turned around that I can't be certain I would even come across those. So, with that logic in mind, I grab my stick and start navigating my way down the ridge. The sun is just starting to peek through the trees, so I think it's still early afternoon but with the storm clouds, it is hard to tell. A slight mist has begun to creep its way in, giving the forest a spooky look. Hopefully, the sun will break through more of the clouds and burn the mist off and it won't be too big of a problem. I glance around and find a small game trail winding its way down the edge of the hillside. I pick my way through the brush, using my stick to push a lot of it out of my way, trying to avoid getting my bad leg stuck. There isn't much pain in the leg anymore, not from the gash that is starting to get a color tinge to it that is concerning, or from the break I am still choosing not to look at. The splint is doing its job in keeping the leg mostly straight. I am not sure if the lack of pain is a good thing or a bad thing, but for now, I am focusing on escaping the forest.

The sun is fully up when I decide to take a break. Another wave of hunger twists through my stomach, and the pain is so intense that I bend over, trying to find some relief. I find a large rock to rest against, pushing the hair out of my face as I do.

My head is pounding from what I'm sure is a mixture of a concussion and dehydration. The mist from earlier in the morning has settled in, turning into a thick fog. This, and my pounding head, makes it harder to focus on my steps, and I nearly fall several times. Luckily, I was somehow able to maintain my balance and keep I going.

It's a relief finding a rock large enough to sit on without having to sink down to the ground. I doubt I'd have the strength to get back up if I sat down too low. I take this opportunity to look around at my new surroundings. I made some good distance on my trek downhill, and the ground has started to level out. It is still a slight grade, but not as much as before. The trees all around me are dead, burned many years ago in a huge forest fire that took weeks to fully contain. Unfortunately, the fire was so big and took up so much area that I'm still not sure where I am. I could still be close to where we had all been yesterday, or I could be miles away. The fire had been huge; I remembered hearing about it on the news one morning before school. They had talked about the large impact on the animal population, and what that had meant for the whole forest's ecosystem. It had all been super sad to listen to the devastation it had caused. Several firefighters who had volunteered from neighboring districts had even been hurt when they were trying to contain it. I'm remembering the news lady describing the scene when I hear a snap behind me.

I whip my head toward the sound as quickly as I can, and my vision swims slightly from the quick movement. As it clears, I scan the tree line behind me, but nothing is there. The lack of living plants makes it slightly easier to see than when I was in the dense forest, but the fog is causing shapes and shadows to distort.

"Stupid squirrels," I grumble, hoping that if I play it off as something small, then maybe I won't panic. I go back to looking around. The snapping goes again, but closer this time. I slowly stand and look around, but again, I see nothing, no movement. But a sense of dread slowly starts to fill me and my heartbeat picks up. It's the same feeling you get when you're walking home alone and you're sure there's someone following you.

"It's just a squirrel," I chant to myself. Grabbing my stick, I slowly start to make my way forward again, angling to the denser area of the forest. All I want to do is get out of the open, to shake this feeling of being exposed. I look back several times, but I see nothing following. I let out the deep breath I had been holding and start hopping my way back down the hill, continuing my trek and praying I find a road or person soon.

…………

The sun is getting higher, and I am getting slower. I haven't found any clean drinking water since this morning and the dehydration is starting to take its toll. My head is still pounding from the possible concussion, and it feels huge, like a balloon has been inflated with lead inside my skull. My lips are dry and cracked, and every now and again I can taste blood. My left leg stopped hurting long ago, which I'm still sure is a bad thing, but for the sake of my sanity, I'm going to take it as a good thing for now.

I've been walking for hours, though I have made very little progress since my rest on the big rock. The rain clouds have begun to grow darker, promising rain that just won't fall. I'm so dehydrated, I have yet to sweat the entire time I've been hiking, even though my lungs are laboring harder and harder. I am almost certain I am being followed now, too, but by what, I'm unsure. It's never far behind, even though I can't see it… but I can sense it. The occasional crack of a branch or the shuffle of lower shrubs is my reminder it is there.

My mind and body are at war with each other. My mind wants me to keep going and to not stop, but my body has reached its limit. It's now been over twenty-four hours since I fell all of which with very little food and several hours with no water. Not to mention the blood I lost, and now that the gash on my leg has reopened slightly, I am starting to lose blood again. But still, I keep myself moving …I have to keep moving. Even the thing behind me has also grown quiet, and I nearly forgot it was there in the first place.

I soon find myself looking for another good spot to rest. The ground has turned rockier and it is taking more thought to move my feet. Several times, my stick lodges itself between two rocks and gets stuck. Rocks that appear stable loosen themselves as soon as my boot touches it. Sliding and stumbling while trying to unwedge my stick from cracks and crevices is not only exhausting but frustrating. The constant state of unbalance strains my muscles that are already screaming in protest from the lack of water. Every minute is a constant battle to stay upright.

Darker thoughts start working their way into my head once again. *What would happen if I just let myself fall? Is it really worth it… trying this hard? I mean, it's inevitable, isn't it? No one is out here. It feels like I have climbed all over this hillside, and I have not seen a single sign of anyone else out here.*

These thoughts are making it very hard to continue. And the longer I am out here the harder they are to shake. Obviously, I know I can't give up hope. I have absolute faith that Chris is out here searching for me and that he will find me. Even if no one else is out here, I know he is. That hope, over all else, is what keeps me going, even now as I face my breaking point.

Spotting a fallen trunk which is the perfect height to sit, I slowly move toward it, keeping my eyes down to watch my step.

I don't even hear it; my brain is so focused on not tripping that I am completely caught off guard when something extremely large and heavy tackles me to the ground. I feel my head smack on the same rocks I had been so careful to walk over a moment ago. The air rushes out of my lungs with a loud *swoosh*. My vision darkens from the impact, the world spinning back into focus. I struggle to regain the breath I lost, gasping and sputtering in the dirt. I try to suck in air, but my chest won't expand. An extremely heavy weight is pressing me into the ground, pinning me there. There is a sudden pain in my left shoulder, like a hundred knives are ripping into me all at once. I finally find air as I let out a loud scream. I suck in, gasping the air now filling my lungs. I let out another scream as whatever has me gripped by the shoulder starts trying to drag me away.

Chapter Seventeen

Chloe

I start fighting, crawling at the ground with my free hand. My lethargic body suddenly finds a renewed sense of energy as adrenaline pumps through my system, trying to keep me alive. I kick and claw at the ground, turning up loose leaves, rocks and dirt as my body is dragged a few more feet. Whatever this thing is, it's incredibly strong since my resistance has little effect on it. I lift my head to let loose another scream, but it chokes in my throat when I see what's right in front of my face. Giant tan paws stand on the ground in front of me, each one bigger than both of my hands combined. It takes another step, dragging me a few more inches. With each backward step it takes, long, sharp claws grab at the earth, using them to ground it firmer and get more leverage to pull me. I glance up from the paws and see matching thick legs rippling with muscles. My gaze tracks up further, finding a massively lean and equally muscular body. The animal is wet and muddy from the rain, but that just makes it all the more terrifying. An image flashes in my mind of the sign I had seen at the beginning of the trailhead. A cougar, that's what has me. The only thing I can't see is the head, which is what it is using to pull me.

The pain is so intense now, I'm surprised I am still conscious. I can feel each tooth pierce through me as it tightens its hold on my shoulder. The protest of every muscle and ligament in my shoulder is almost unbearable as the cougar pulls me across the rocky terrain. I turn my head slightly and I see the powerful jaw clamped tightly over my entire shoulder. The fur around the mouth crinkles from needing to be open so far, and a slight glint of the base of its teeth can be seen as he readjusts his grip. The sight is so terrifying, and I try screaming again, but my mouth is so dry that I barely make any noise. I can feel its breath on the back of my neck as it labors to pull my weight out of the clearing and into the cover of the trees.

The cougar continues dragging me for a couple more yards before it finally releases me. The teeth pull out of my arm, allowing me to find my voice and let out a loud scream. The fog still swirls around, which seems to work its way into my brain, and my vision blurs for a moment.

This is it... He's going to eat me. This is how I'm going to die… face down in a mud puddle, in the middle of a forest. They probably won't even find my body. Do cougars eat bones?

My mind starts to float off into other directions as I lay here, waiting, for the cougar to end it, but nothing happens. I can't even feel his breath on my neck anymore. Sticks snap somewhere nearby, but I continue to stay still. Is that what you're supposed to do when a cougar attacks? Or are you supposed to fight? I can't remember, but this isn't really something they teach you in biology class. And my guidebook had been more about viewing nature, not what to do when nature attacks.

My body ends up making the decision for me. The pain and the exhaustion are so crippling, it is all I can do to just breathe in and out. I stay laying there until I can't stand it another minute, and I have to look. Gritting my teeth and moving slowly, I pull my right hand under my chest and use my good leg to push myself over. I feel my left arm drag and then lay limply at my side, with blood and dirt smearing all down it, staining the ground from where I had been laying in one spot for so long. I don't even look at my shoulder; I just can't handle anymore. I had already endured the sight of my broken leg, and I'm not sure I would even want to continue if I looked at where the cougar had bitten me. Although, it doesn't hurt as much as it had before, which triggers a small part of my brain as being odd. I can feel the sticky warmth of the blood seeping out of the wound, though, so I know without looking that the injury is bad. My vision is blurry again and darkness creeps around the edges, but I have to see where it is, to see if the animal is sitting, watching me, waiting to attack again and finish what it started.

Craning my neck to lift my head up, I scan the area, but the cougar is nowhere in sight. *Where has it gone?* Is he waiting in the trees for me to die before coming back for me? Slowly, I lower my head back to the ground and wrack my memory for any facts that may have been on that sign from the start of the hike that I might have retained. Mentally, I kick myself for not taking it more seriously or doing any research on the dangerous wildlife up here before this trip.

Sticks crack again slightly off to my right, and my pulse spikes as my head whips around in response, but there is nothing but trees. Breath still whooshes in and out of my mouth in small gasps as I let my eyes drift back up to the sky. Small white clouds float across the light blue sky, with more dark rain clouds trailing behind them. Or was that just my vision turning them dark and stormy? The sun that broke through is hot on my face, which feels nice after being stuck in the dark trees, soaked with rain. I lick my cracked lips, trying to get some relief, but my dry tongue just scratches along the rough skin.

Cracking sounds again, this time behind me. I crane my head back, trying to see. The world slowly shifts upside down, and I realize this position causes my throat to jut forward, completely exposed to any predators, but I no longer care. I would rather look death in the face as it comes for me. I scan the trees, the dark rings around my vision throwing strange shadows near the edges. But I can still make out a form emerging from the edge of the tree line. My breath catches as a tan body on four legs gracefully takes a few steps into the clearing. The animal takes a few more steps, and by doing so, brings itself into focus. Confusion contorts my brain as the animal's shape doesn't really match the body I was envisioning. The fog in my head prevents me from firmly latching on to the animal's name. This creature's legs are tall and thin, not strong and muscular. Its chest is narrow, not broad. No large paws with curved claws dig into the earth as it prowls forward, but small dainty hoofs that make just a slight muffled *knock* as it steps. This time the name doesn't escape me. I latch onto it, holding it there, chanting it in my brain. *It's a deer. This animal is a deer. It's just a deer.* Calmness settles through me as I realize this isn't a large hungry cat back to claim its meal, but a small doe, carefully stepping around the rocks, getting nearer and nearer to me. She's now made her way closer to my right side, and I relax my shoulders, bringing my head back down slightly and shifting so I can still see her. My movement catches the deer's attention and she pauses, looking at me intently, just as I did moments earlier with her, trying to determine if I am a threat. Her large brown eyes lock onto mine. I suddenly understand the expression 'doe eyed.' They are so perfectly round and full of a gentleness that I don't think I have ever seen in another living creature's eyes before.

A memory from a few days ago comes to mind, of the deer by the lake. The single doe who had looked up at me with eyes similar to this one. *I wonder if it's the same one?* I know deer can move very quickly, so it could be the same one. Another memory surfaces of many years ago, during one of the only times my dad took us on vacation. We had gone camping in a small trailer he had borrowed from a family friend. He had dragged us on a hike to go see some waterfall that was 'only a mile or two' up on the trail, which ended up being more like five or six miles. But on the way up there we had startled some small deer that were bedded down off the side of the trail, and they had shot up like rockets and bounded into the trees so quickly, Mom hadn't even seen them.

I'm roused from my stream of daydreams and memories when the deer in front of me suddenly shifts. Her ears twitch, picking up a sound that less sensitive human ears can't detect. Her gaze raises from mine and looks into the trees on the other side of the clearing. I am too tired to follow her gaze.; besides, I know exactly what she hears, even without hearing it myself. Large, padded feet falling onto the damp earth. Maybe a stick or two breaking under the sheer weight of the mountain cat. Maybe this was its plan all along… To sit in the shadows and wait for something else to get curious over the smell of blood, wandering into a trap themselves. Then it would bound in here and finish us both off. But deer are fast, so maybe she could make it out. She didn't appear injured; she didn't have to die here with me. I continue to just watch her while her eyes continue their sweep of the tree line. Her ears move like little satellite dishes on her head, swiveling this way and that, trying to pick up anything that sounds like danger. I watch her, my vision worsening by the minute, darkening little by little. Soon she too will be out of focus, just like the trees behind her are now.

A shuffling noise comes from behind me, which is close enough that even my ears hear it. This seems to be what the doe has been waiting for. Slowly, she turns away from me and starts making her way back into the forest, back into safety. She moves with a swiftness that is both quick and silent as her hooved feet don't even stumble as she makes her way over the rocky ground. Within seconds, she is just another color blended into my field of vision. The forest has become a watercolor painting, with every color blending into the next. A small tear runs down my cheek into the dirt as the only companion I'd had over the last day and a half -and probably my last ever- leaves me.

I go back to looking at the sky as my sight grows darker until another shadow passes over me. *This is it; he's finally back to finish what he started.* I close my eyes as thoughts of my family flash through my mind. Feelings of how much I love Chris and my mom and my brother and sister. Will Lilly remember me? Or will I be just another family member people tell her about? Another smiling face hanging on the wall, just a memory. Ethan will never make it out of his goth phase now. My poor mother… Who will be her rock now? I had been the one that got her through my dad's death. I'm the one who held her when she cried, fed Lilly on those days and nights when she simply couldn't get herself out of bed. Who will be there for her when I'm gone? More silent tears stream down my cheeks. *I miss her so much.* Since the moment I had awoken at the bottom of this god damn mountain, I tried my hardest to keep all thoughts of them at bay. But now I let myself think of them. Think of Lilly's laughter when she gets good and giggly, and Ethan's laughter in those odd moments when he lets his guard down while he plays with her. Of the feeling of my mom's arms around me in a hug that only a mom could give. I think of Chris's hand in mine when we are walking side by side. Every moment of our life together flashes through my thoughts. Every touch, every kiss, every fight, every laugh I did at his stupid jokes… I let myself think of them all and allow the sadness and the ache of missing them engulf me.

My mind is in complete turmoil as I internally fall apart and mentally say goodbye to the ones I love most in this whole world. I can tell even with closed eyes that the shadow moves closer, blocking the sunlight as it covers more ground. Heavy footfalls sound so close, I can almost feel their vibrations across the rocks that lay under me. I open my eyes, hoping for one last look at the sky when a face suddenly appears over mine but not the face of an animal. It is the face of a man...

Chapter Eighteen

Tom

Seeing Chloe the other day had been nice, even though she had spilled soda all down my shirt. It had brought back fond memories of when we were younger. She had always been awkward as a kid; her legs grew so fast, she seemed to always be tripping over something. We had been really good friends until high school, but we had drifted apart. I had gotten into football and swim team and she had been on track. We both hung out with a different friend group, and took different classes, but we saw each other in the halls, and always seemed to have the same English teacher. Those had been good memories but now…now was not going to be a good memory. The news had spread fast, and when I heard she had been in some kind of accident on the mountain and was missing, I was one of the first to volunteer to help find her.

I ran home and threw all my first aid gear into a pack I now carried with me, and I was assigned to Chris's group, along with his and Chloe's group of friends. The search and rescue team had been able to get a general idea of where the ledge she fell off would end, but there were so many ridges that fingered off, that we had been searching all through the night. Our search range was very broad especially since, if she had survived and was trying to get out, we knew she could have wandered even farther out. Even with half the town out here looking, it could take days to cover it all.

I kept a close eye on Chris as well as looking for Chloe, and I saw his friends were doing the same. He seemed to be under the impression that it was his fault she was missing. Just by watching his face, I knew the turmoil was eating at him by the hour. As the night went on, he became more crazed, his head whipping around at any noise. But no matter what anyone said, he just kept charging ahead, never wanting to take a break. Sometimes I'd catch him take her picture out and stare at it, which seemed to renew his energy because he'd take a long breath before gently sliding it back into the chest pocket of his jacket, surging forward again.

In the beginning, we would hear small updates on the radio. Nothing big, just people checking off one grid or another. Then, as we expanded the search, we would hear fewer and fewer check-ins. After a few hours of hearing nothing on the radio, Chris kept pulling it out of his pocket and checking it every few minutes to see if it was working. And then the rain had started. Even with it pouring down around us, it just seemed to urge Chris on faster. And I, for one, couldn't blame him; the rain was coming down so hard, it was for sure going to wipe any trail Chloe might have left. Any chance we had of tracking her was long gone. Our only hope now was hearing something or stumbling right into her.

We searched for hours with no hint that Chloe had ever been there, and our moods grew darker and darker. It wasn't until an hour before dawn that Chris agreed to head back to base camp. And he only did because Bill was piggy-backing Martha after another fall, Fred was getting really irritable, and we were all severely caked in mud and soaked through.

Once at the base camp, the sun was already rising and just as many people were leaving the woods as were going back in. Bill and Fred had crawled into one of their rigs and were trying to catch some sleep. Martha had a shift at the hospital that due to the lack of cell service she couldn't get covered, so she headed back into town. I was hanging next to Chris, drinking my second cup of coffee, when someone finally came over the radio. "Hey, chief, we've found a backpack matching the description of the one Chloe was wearing. There's no sign of her, but we have our starting point of where she fell and landed."

Dropping his coffee, Chris lunged at the radio he had set down next to the coffee pot. "What are your coordinates?"

The man on the other end relayed his position, and with me trailing behind, Chris took off back into the woods. It wasn't long before Bill and Fred came crashing after us.

It took us a few hours to get to where the backpack had been found. The mountain grew steep, and we were both out of breath by the time we reached the small search team who had found the bag. The backpack was soaked and had mud caked all over it, along with dark spots we all knew were blood but chose to ignore. The man had been right when he said there was no sign of her. No footprints, no path, nothing. The rain had done the one thing we had feared it would… it wiped any trace that she had been there. There were signs that something had come through here fast as plants had upturned and rocks had been disturbed. But if you walked a few feet in either direction, it looked like the same thing had happened everywhere. The excess rain that had fallen had caused mud slides down the steep hillside. The backpack was found in a place where it could have been thrown from any location.

After the backpack was found and we saw how many directions she could have gone, we decided to split up. We would cover more ground separate than we would if we were together. Each of us branched off in a different direction she might have wandered. The only slightly reassuring sign was that we hadn't found a body at the bottom of the hill. So, she had been alive after the fall, she had made it and was uninjured enough to get up and walk away. But she had been missing for almost a day now and a lot could have happened between then and now.

I had been reluctant to let Chris go off on his own. Now that I could see him better, he wasn't looking so good. His hair was all out of place, his clothes a mess from hiking through the woods, getting rained on, and then the clothes drying all muddy. He looked exhausted, and his eyes, though alert with hope, were also hollow. But he hadn't waited for me; he just picked a direction and headed off, not waiting for anyone to follow or stop him. Because Chris had gone off downhill to the left, I decided to take the right. Several other people had gone in the same direction, but each of us angled and broke off separate from the group.

I yelled Chloe's name until my throat was hoarse. The rain had been a menace throughout the day, a constant drizzle filtering down from dark clouds through the trees. There were bits of ground that had been disturbed here and there, but it was hard to tell if it was caused by a human, animal, or from the elements.

As I continue hiking, the ground slowly starts leveling out, but I can still tell I'm going downhill though there is very little slope. The trees here are getting more and more sparse, and I soon realize that the trees are becoming drier, until every tree around me is nothing more than tall standing shells.

All the trees, if you can call them that, are black and gray as I enter a clearing. "This must be the beginning of the burn area," I whisper, feeling like I'm in a grave-yard. The air feels heavy, and just a general eerie feeling seems to envelop everything around me. Birds that I had grown used to flitting from one tree to the other have all but disappeared. Small patches of grass have begun to grow again, adding a touch of color to an otherwise bland landscape. Even the rustle of the leaves in the wind or the swish of my pant legs seemed too loud. I take another step into the clearing, and as I'm debating about crossing the clearing or not, a scream pierces the quiet of the forest. The sound echoes off the hollow bodies of the trees.

"Chloe!" Turning, I start running in the direction I heard the scream from. "Chloe!" I yell again, racing through the trees, pushing branches out of my way as they snap against my hands, arms, and face as I climb over deadfall. I slow down so I can listen.

"Come on," I whisper. "Come on, make a noise... Tell me where you are." I slow to a stop, trying to figure out if I'm going the right way or not. I twist my head from side to side, hoping to pick up some kind of noise again or see some sign of her.

The forest is darker in this area. The trees are so closely packed that even though they don't have leaves you can barely see the sun or the sky. This is why the fire caused so much damage. It wouldn't have been hard for the fire to jump from one tree to another until the whole forest was up in flames.

I glance at my watch; it is getting later in the evening and soon, it will be dark outside of the tree line. I take my pack off and dig around until I can find my flashlight and switch it on while swinging the pack back onto my shoulders. The flashlight beam is bright enough to see where I am walking, but fallen trees and new, untamed underbrush cause shadowed areas and the last thing I want to do is accidentally walk right past her and not even know.

The scream I had heard earlier still echoes through my mind. That was not a scream of frustration or to alert someone to where you are. That was the kind of scream one did when something was truly undoubtedly wrong. It was the one your body makes all on its own, when it's filled with pain and fear. The hair on the back of my neck is still on end from the memory of it.

I move my flashlight beam through the shadowed areas around me, careful to not miss anything. As I'm scanning the last shadows near me, another yell rings out, this one quieter, more strangled, but unquestionably coming close to the left of me. I turn and run deeper into the trees, hoping I can find her.

Chapter Nineteen

Tom

I'm running again, throwing myself over logs and across the uneven ground. I'm yelling out Chloe's name when the snapping of branches makes me come to a stop so fast, I almost fall over. My head's on a swivel looking for her, looking for a blonde-haired girl stumbling around in the woods. I'm looking so hard for her, I almost missed the huge cat stalking through the bushes. My hands go cold, and my heart is beating about a hundred miles a minute. It's staring at me intently; he's filthy and covered in mud, and by his hunched shoulders and dropped head, an obvious hunting stance. I know he's hungry. But the predator has lost the element of surprise, and I'm not going to let him get the upper hand. "Get out of here!" I yell, trying to scare it off. I square my shoulders to bring myself up to my full height, and throw my hands out to my sides. "Go on! I said get out of here!" I'm tempted to throw my flashlight, but it's the heavy, durable kind, and if he decides to attack, it would be more help in my hand.

After a few seconds, the cat starts backing away, his gaze never leaving mine. As he turns, a stream of light from the setting sun breaks through the trees and rain clouds, highlighting his fur. Along with the mud caked on his head, there is also something shining red and it's not partially dry like the mud beneath it, so I know it's fresh. My chest tightens at the possibilities. The large cat finally turns, and as he is just about hidden in the shadows, I catch a peek at the rest of his body before my view is completely obstructed. Ribs poke out of his muscled side, patches of muddy fur missing. *The only thing scarier than a cougar is a sick cougar. There's no telling what he is willing to do to survive.*

I wait till he's completely out of sight before going in the direction he had come from. I can feel in my gut this isn't a coincidence, no matter how many times I chant in my head that it is. The scream I heard earlier, and now seeing the mountain lion is too much of a coincidence.

With a sickening feeling curling in my stomach, I approach the edge of another clearing.

....

I can see her already; she's laying face up. Her eyes are open, staring up at the sky. The shock of seeing her causes me to pause for just a moment. From where I am standing, I can't tell if she's alive or not. My shock wears off after a moment, and I take off running at full speed, trying to get to her as fast as I can. I breathe a sigh of relief when I see her chest move as I get closer. I drop to my knees when I reach her, half sliding to a stop. Her eyes are open wide, and when she sees my face, she visibly relaxes. "Tom…" she whispers, her voice cracking."Yeah, it's me, Chloe. You're going to be alright now, okay?" Her eyes suddenly look glazed and unfocused, but her mouth is open, so I can hear her breathing, but it's in shallow gasps.

"Chloe… can you hear me? Chloe!"

I move to scoop her up, and that's when I see the blood. I have been so focused on getting to her that I hadn't fully looked at her. But now I can see her leg is swollen and tied up with what appears to be a makeshift splint. And her shoulder; I have seen some pretty nasty cuts before, but her shoulder has nearly been torn off. My mind flashes back to the cougar I had seen earlier. There is no doubt in my mind now that he had been the cause of this.

I take off my backpack and pull my sweatshirt out. I examine the wound closer. It's deep and though blood flows freely from it, blocking my view below the skin, there is a definite pattern of teeth from the cougar. Nothing else could have made a bite like that. I start wrapping the sweatshirt around her shoulder gently, trying to staunch the bleeding. While doing so, I do a quick check of the rest of her. Her face, though scratched and bruised, seems fine. Her lips are so cracked from dehydration, dried blood settles at the corners. I pull my water bottle from my bag and gently lift it to her mouth while trying to support her head in my other hand. Her mouth purses when the water hits her lips, but she doesn't attempt to swallow any of the water. I throw the bottle back into the bag and grab the walkie-talkie that, until now, has been dead silent.

"Can anyone hear me?" I call into it, hoping I am not too far out of range of the others.

"Tom?" Chris's voice comes through.

"Hey… I've got her. She's alive, but badly hurt. She has a leg that she's bandaged herself up pretty good… looks like it's broken. And she was attacked by a cougar. She's losing a lot of blood, so be ready when we come out."

"Where are you? I'll meet you there." I can hear the desperation in Chris' voice. I'm sure he is gripping the walkie-talkie in his hands, clutching it like a life-line.

"I'm not one hundred percent sure of my coordinates, and there's no time to wait for you. I know how I got in here but not enough to walk you in. Don't worry Chris, I'll get her out of here."

"Thank you, Tom." A female voice, Chloe's mom, comes over the radio.

I don't wait to see if Chris tries to argue any further, but my guess is Mrs. Whiteshed's comment ended any further debate. I throw the walkie-talkie back into the backpack and pull the straps over my shoulders.

"Alright, Chloe, we need to get you out of here."

Shuffling around to her right side, I carefully scoop her into my arms, trying my best to jostle her as little as possible. Her face contorts into a pained expression and a moan escapes from her mouth, but once she settles in my arms, her body goes limp again.

I start the hike out of this damn forest, and luckily, my first aid and safety training I had to take for my job kicks in. I just start talking, trying to give her something to focus on, something to keep her awake. I continue talking to her the whole time I'm moving through the trees. I tell her updates on how much farther we have to go, and I point out birds and wildlife. I get a small glimmer of attention when I mention a deer who is grazing in a small clearing we pass, but for the most part, her eyes are unfocused, not really paying attention to what I am saying, until I mention Chris. Her eyes snap to mine with laser focus. I fill her in on how he pulled the town together to come find her, and how he had barely taken a single break the whole time. I tell her anything and everything I can think of that might interest her about the time I spent with him the last day and a half. I also start rolling through names of everyone else who is out looking for her that she may know.

Luckily, the burned-out area isn't far from basecamp, and we don't find any steep inclines, so even with carrying Chloe, we make good time.

"Almost there, Chloe…" I whisper to her. "Almost there."

Chapter Twenty

Chloe

Tom's face came first as a shock. Seeing him surrounded by a halo of pine trees and sky was so alien. It was not the face I had been expecting. But slowly, the surprise and confusion melted away into relief. They had been looking for me. All my negative, dark thoughts had been wrong. And now I've been found. It may be too late, but at least my family will have closure if it is. His face disappears and I can hear him rummage around in something, a bag I am guessing. There is some pressure on my shoulder, but no pain. The pain has dulled to a throb in the background of my mind. Tom then slowly props my head up, and I can see the rim of a water bottle. The minute the water hit my lips, I could have cried in relief. The flood of cool water instantly sooths the dryness on my lips that has been a constant irritation. I try to swallow some, but my throat is so dry and my tongue has gone numb, so the water just trickles down my chin. I can hear the sounds of male voices. Tom's and someone else's. But I can't see anyone else around me, nor can I make out much of what he is saying. Tom's shadow passes over me and I feel him slowly move his arms under me.

When he first lifts me into his arms, it hurts so bad, I am sure I am going to pass out. That dull throb of pain had sunken in the back of my consciousness burst back through and lit up every part of my body like a Christmas tree. A gasp was even able to make its way through my dry, swollen throat. But Tom's arms are strong, and he holds me so steady that I barely shift after the initial lift and the pain dulls back down again.

I can hear him talking to me as he walks saying how close I am to some place called basecamp, and he mentions birds and the scenery we pass. When he mentions a deer he sees, I can't help but wonder if it's my deer?

But it isn't until he gets to Chris that I really tune in. I am going to see Chris again. An hour ago, I had resigned myself to the fact that he was gone forever, and I would never get to tell him how much I loved him, but now I would.

Tom's description worries me, though. It sounds like Chris has barely even blinked since my fall. I can't imagine what this has done to him, to my family. Tom mentions them too, letting me know my mom and Ethan are out here somewhere. A tightness constricts my chest. Is this just guilt over putting them all through this settling into my chest, making it harder to breathe, or is this something else? A small alarm bell chimes in my head but I try to ignore it.

I am impressed by Tom's strength. Not once has he had to sit or put me down at all. His breath comes out in small huffs but other than that, he shows no signs of exhaustion or fatigue. The sun is setting when we finally break through the last of the trees, making the sky look like it is on fire. The storm clouds that seem to just circle the forest wherever I am glow in the last light of the day. They slowly move in, blocking the final rays of sunshine, turning the sky black. A few raindrops splash onto my cheeks, and they feel cool against my skin. I can hear all kinds of noise in the direction we are walking, lots of shouting. A few voices stand out more than others, their tones familiar. I can hear my mother, her voice hysterical and gradually getting louder. Soon, it is directly next to me, her face moving in and out of my line of sight. Tom never slows down, though, not until we reach the ambulance.

Red lights flash above me, more raindrops reflecting in the rays of light. There is so much noise in comparison to the quiet forest I just left that I feel like my eardrums are about to explode from the sudden change. So much is happening. So many sounds, voices, and lights. The world starts whirling and blending together as my brain gradually begins to feel lighter and lighter. I hear another familiar voice that momentarily pulls me out of my trance. My heart flutters right before I am transferred from Tom's arms into another set Chris's. His worried expression appears over my face. His eyes lock onto mine for a split second before he looks up and begins shouting orders at the surrounding paramedics before laying me down on a gurney. I groan, not only from the jostling, but from not wanting him to let me go yet. Chris, hearing my noise, must mistake it as a groan of pain, and he hurries even more.

I am quickly strapped in and hauled into the ambulance, though my eyes never leave Chris's face. The big doors slam shut behind me, instantly silencing the roar of sound. As I lie there, I can feel the stinging pain of needles poking into my arm and other equipment quickly being attached.

There is a tugging feeling at my shoulder, and I glance over to see Chris pulling away whatever Tom had used to bind my shoulder. I catch a glimpse of it from the corner of my eye before it is discarded to the floor. A large black sweatshirt, completely soaked in blood, is quickly tossed away from my sight. I move my gaze to Chris's face, trying to gauge how bad it is, but his expression is like a mask. Every instinct I have wants me to look at my shoulder, to see what he sees, but a small, rational part of me still knows like it did on that mountain that if I do look, I won't be able to handle what I see.

Chris soon has scissors in his hand and is cutting away at what's left of my shirt. The shredded material falls away in pieces, softly hitting the ambulance floor. His mouth is moving, and I suddenly realize he's talking, but I can no longer hear him. I hadn't noticed after the sound from the outside was cut off that I wasn't hearing any noise from the guys working on me. There had been no slap when the soiled sweatshirt hit the floor. No beeping from the monitors whose wires snaked around and are stuck to various parts of me. A whirring noise in my ears has replaced all other sounds. Panic grips my insides as it becomes slightly harder to breathe. My chest feels tight, and my head is so foggy that it feels like a cloud-filled bowling ball laying on the thin padding of the gurney. I can no longer feel the needles or the tugging. The shadows bordering around my vision become darker and darker until I think my eyes have actually closed. It all came on so slowly, I hadn't noticed, but once I did start to notice, it engulfed me all at once. Just as everything is becoming all muddled together, a lightness begins to fill me. The pressure in my head slowly slips away, along with all my other pain. It feels nice, warm and peaceful. Completely silent too, until a noise rips through the peace.

Someone is yelling at me. Apparently, my hearing isn't gone entirely because I can definitely tell the voice is angry and does not belong in the lightness all around me. I can't understand what the angry voice is saying though, but it doesn't matter, because it's growing fainter and fainter until…

It's gone.

Chapter Twenty-One

Chris

Complete chaos erupted the moment Tom stepped through the trees carrying Chloe. Mrs. Whiteshed had taken off at a dead sprint, and everyone else just started yelling either in excitement, or into walkie-talkies, relaying the news that she had been found and everyone could start their hikes out. I, on the other hand, rooted myself in place by the ambulance, waiting for Tom to get closer so I could take her. Every part of me wanted to run to her like her mother, but I knew I would be more help here. Even though I was out of uniform, my boss had more or less made an exception that I could work in the ambulance Chloe was in when we found her.

Basically, I told him I would be, and he didn't fight me on it.

Bill and Fred had both rested long enough earlier in the day that the chief allowed them to pick up the shift of staying with the ambulance parked at basecamp, allowing the other shift to go home and rest. Both of them were currently standing by my side, waiting. With the unpredictability of the storms circling overhead, there was no way an emergency helicopter could get in to fly her out. So, the ambulance would have to do. I spare a glance up at the sky as another storm is just starting to unleash itself on us.

When Tom finally gets to me, it is all I can do to keep myself standing. Her whole shoulder is covered in a very large sweatshirt that, at one point, had been gray. The whole thing, now soaked in blood, has turned a blackish-red shade, except for a few small areas where the original color is still visible. I look up into Tom's face and give him a nod of thanks before taking Chloe from his arms. I am careful not to bring her too close to my body. Even though her injuries are extensive, it is her face I can't keep my eyes off of even if it doesn't look like the face I remember. It is a face I feared I would never see again. I rake my eyes over it, taking in every detail. Her skin is so white, it makes her eyes seem as big as saucers, her lips are dry and cracked, and her once blonde hair is now caked in mud and in a tangle around her head. Her eyes, the one feature that seems unchanged by the mountain, lock onto mine immediately.

As much as I want to just stand there and hold her, she needs my help more. I turn and yell at Fred to start an I.V. line and to get ready to start flushing out the cuts and scratches. Gently, I lay her on the gurney the guys had pulled out as soon as she got close. A small gasp escapes her, and I can't tell if it's from pain and if so, from where. Quickly, I strap her in and start pushing the bed into the back of the ambulance. Fred grabs the other end and together, we get her in and close the door. Bill is up front driving, and I feel the lurch forward as we start off down the road, sirens blaring. Fred's already got her I.V. going and an oxygen mask hooked over her mouth and nose, and then he moves to hook her up to the heart monitor. His face is completely blank, like I know mine should be. It will only make it ten times harder if I let my emotions get the better of me. It's hard, but I steel myself and clench my jaw before I move over to her shoulder and begin peeling away Tom's huge sweatshirt.

The trauma is severe and the only thing I can think of that could have caused this much damage is a huge animal. I know Tom had said she had been attacked by an animal, but nothing could have prepared me for this. Whatever creature that did this had almost taken her arm completely off. The wounds are so deep, I can see bone. The teeth had cleanly ripped through the muscle, tendons, and ligaments. Which, as strange as it sounds, is a small blessing; it will make it much easier for it to heal cleanly.

Her shirt is practically nonexistent, but there are still parts that have to be cut away to keep them from getting in any of the wounds and causing any problems. I reach behind me for the scissors and begin snipping away the shirt. I can feel Chloe's eyes on me, and I know she is scared; I also know that I am wound so tight that if I look at her face again, I'll snap and completely come undone.

The last pieces of the shirt are finally removed, and I am draping a medical blanket over her to save Fred from seeing so much of his friend when the tempo of the beeping from her heart monitor starts to slow. For the first time since I started working, I look at Chloe's face. Her skin is paler than before, but it's her eyes with their almost vacant look, that makes my heart want to stop right along with hers. "Chloe!" I shout. "Chloe! No, no, no Chloe! Stay with me." I start chest compressions while Fred pushes epinephrine into the I.V. trying to get her heart beating faster, but it's no use. The beeping keeps getting slower until it flatlines. "She's going into cardiac arrest!" I yell at Fred, who immediately grabs the defibrillator. I yank the blanket to the side, to hell with modesty. Fred hands over the paddles and helps me stick the pads on her skin, one on her right shoulder the other on the left lower side of her chest. His face is stone; he has also pulled himself inward, locking out all emotion, just as I have done. "It's charged and ready when you are." Fred says, pushing a final button on the machine. I can hear the familiar whining of the machine charging. "Clear," I say loudly so he can hear me over the noise. And then I press the paddles onto the pads.

Chloe's body jolts and then is still, the monitor still reading nothing. "Ramping power, charging, clear!" Fred yells.

I press the paddles back down, and Chloe's body jolts again. "Come on baby, come on." I chant, watching the monitor. My eyes are watering so badly that I have to keep blinking to clear them. I hadn't even noticed I was crying, but I know I can't lose her again. Not after I just got her back. I won't. Anger rips through me. Never in the years we have been together have I ever gotten angry with Chloe. We have had disagreements but never any major fights. But now I am furious.

"You come back to me, right now, Chloe Whiteshed! Do you hear me?! You come back right now!" I roar. Doubt starts to creep in that the little red line on the monitor will ever move, but then… it slowly does.

"Chloe?" I yell and turn back to her face, dropping the paddles onto the gurney. Putting a hand on each of her cheeks, I look into her eyes and she blinks at me, the vacancy in her eyes fading away.

"Oh, thank God," I gasp and smooth back her hair. "I thought I lost you again." Her lips form into a broken smile that looks more like a grimace, but her eyes soften. I kiss her forehead before going back to work on her shoulder.

Fred and I are just finishing prepping her for the trauma team when we pull up to the hospital. Thanks to a police escort and Bill driving probably a hundred miles per hour, we had cut the travel time in half. Bill swings the doors open, and then it's chaos. The E.R. staff is rushing out to meet us as we push the gurney through the doors. "Female, age twenty-two, severe trauma to left shoulder and back of neck, broken leg, and possible concussion." Fred's voice rings out as Chloe's face starts blanking again. "Went into cardiac arrest once during transport from either severe blood loss or shock." Fred continues to tell the doctors and nurses what had happened, though they didn't need much catching up. We had alerted the hospital earlier in case she came in with someone else. They had been kept in the loop about how she had gone missing, and they made sure they had a trauma doctor available whenever we brought her in. "Alright, let's get her prepped for surgery. I want her in operating room one," the doctor who seems to be in charge yells. We push her into the prepping area where the nurses cut away the remainder of her clothes. Fred and Bill snap their faces away, looking at various objects on the wall. "You don't have to stay," I say, walking over to them. "You sure? We can stay if you need us to." Bill rests his hand on my shoulder. "Yeah, I'm sure. You two have done enough. I really appreciate it, and I know Chloe does too, so thanks…" My voice cracks at the end. I am barely keeping it together. My nerves feel like a rubber band stretched to near breaking. I am just waiting for the snap and the sharp pain to follow. "No problem. You would have done the same if the situation were reversed," Fred says, giving me a small smile before he turns to leave, with Bill following close behind. I take a deep breath and turn back to Chloe. Her eyes are shut, but as I rush over and grab her hand, I notice the heart monitor is still going strong. "What happened?" I ask, turning to the closest nurse. "We sedated her. Unless you want her to lose the arm, we have to get her into surgery," she says and grabs the rails of the hospital bed. They must have transferred her while my back was turned. I help them push her down the hall until we reach the doors to the operating room. "I'm sorry, you can't go any farther," one of the nurses who was in the room says putting a hand on my chest to stop me. I turn to face her, ready to argue, but I instantly deflate when I see the nurse is Martha.

I turn and watch as the other nurses push Chloe through the doors. It slowly swings shut, and my crossed arms fall limply to my sides. "I will personally do everything I can. I promise you," Martha reassures me as she slowly draws her hand down and grabs mine, giving it a gentle squeeze. We just stand there until the door bursts open again, and one of the other nurses' hurries from the room. When the door starts swinging again, I get glimpses of a doctor standing over Chloe, doing chest compressions. Her heart stopped… again. "Martha, we need you in there, now!" the nurse yells, running back into the room pushing a cart.

"Martha? Martha what's going on? Is she okay?" I can hear my voice grow louder as I make for the door.

She pushes me back. "You have to stay out here. You hear me, Chris? You stay right here. I will fill you in when I can." And with that, she makes her way into the room. A slight limp from her wrapped ankle keeps her from the full run the other nurses were moving with, though I can feel her urgency to help Chloe. The sight reminds me that she had been out there with us. I wonder what story she spun to her supervisor to allow her in there?

I move closer to the door, trying to glimpse anything I can as a slow, continuous beeping echoes through the hallway. All I can see now is Martha moving over to the sink and more nurses frantically running back and forth.

Chapter Twenty-Two

Chris

I stay outside the door, hoping Martha will come back out, but she never does. I guess it's a good sign, but still, it's hard to leave the door. I don't know when the tears started again, but I can eventually feel them running down my face. I slowly make my way back down the halls that we had rushed down. I stop every few steps to look back at the door, but no one comes back out. After a few more feet, I can't take it anymore, and the tears come faster, making it hard to see. I back up against the wall and sink down, pulling my knees to my chest and burying my face in my arms. The weight of the past several hours suddenly is too much, and I can no longer hold the emotion back.

All the fear, pain, and guilt rushes through me. My fingers rake through my hair as sobs rip their way out of my chest, making my whole-body shake.

"Please…" I gasp. "Please don't take her. Not now, not like this." It's all I can do to get these words out as I silently pray to whoever is listening.

I stay sitting there for a while, even after the crying has stopped. I wait to see if a nurse will kick me out of the hall, especially since I am out of uniform, but no one does. In fact, the halls are completely quiet. There is no chaos, no yelling, no hiking or mud. That is all over; now, there is just the clean, quiet hospital, but the gut-wrenching fear is still as present as ever. The worst part of the waiting is that I can't do anything to help. Like in the forest, my part is over. At least in the forest, I could do something productive. I could help Chloe; I could find her, and then I could get her to safety.

But now I'm useless; I can't do anything more for her. Now it is in the hands of the doctors and nurses, and in Chloe's will to survive. I slide my hand into my jacket pocket and pull out Chloe's photo. It's bent and crinkled, spattered with water from the rain. The top corner is stained red from Chloe's blood that had soaked through my shirt. I stare at the photo like I had done dozens of times on that mountain. I should probably throw this copy away since it's almost completely destroyed; I'm honestly surprised it's still in one piece. But instead, I slip it back into the pocket where it's spent so many hours and zip the pocket closed.

Eventually, I get back on my feet and continue down the hall until I hit the doors for the waiting room. I take a deep breath before pushing them open and walking through. Chloe's mom is pacing across the small room until she sees me and rushes forward. "What's happening? Is she okay? Where is Chloe?"

I take a quick look around the room, spotting Bill and Fred, who are standing in one corner with Tom. It appears as though they had been talking, but stopped when I came in. Ethan is also here, sitting in one of the chairs nearby with Lilly on his lap. So many other people are crammed into the small room, and I recognize a few from the search groups, while others are strangers, waiting for their own loved ones.

"She's in surgery now," I say loud enough for everyone to hear. "I wasn't allowed back there, but Martha said they'll do everything they can for her, but…" I let my voice trail off, unsure if I should tell them all what I saw. Mrs. Whiteshed's eyes fill with tears, and Ethan starts distracting Lilly with a coloring book before she notices. His hands are balled into fists so tight, his knuckles are turning white. I pull Chloe's mom into a hug and lead her to one of the unoccupied chairs.

We sit for what feels like forever. Bill and Fred make several coffee runs down to the cafeteria. Most of us haven't slept since the search first started, still in the same clothes because we haven't gone home yet, either. Lilly is curled in a ball, fast asleep, in a pile of everyone's jackets by her brother's feet. It's a strange sight; she looks so much like Chloe. They have the same hair, almost the same face, but Chloe has more of her dad's features than Lilly, more angular. And here she is, fast asleep, blissfully unaware that her big sister is fighting for her life just a few doors down the hall. What must it be like to still have that kind of innocence? I lean my head back in the chair and close my eyes. The sound of the falling rain outside fills the quiet room. The repetitive drum of it hitting the hospital windows creates a therapeutic rhythm. For the first time in almost two days, I drift off to sleep.

………..

I jerk awake at the sound of the door opening, and I look around to see if I missed anything. The scene around me has changed only slightly. It's still dark outside, the rain nothing more than a small drizzle. Mrs. Whiteshed is still in the chair next to me, quietly talking to someone on her phone. I look back to the door, and a couple around Chloe's mom's age walks in, their shoulders hunched in grief. I feel sorry for them; I know the anguish they are feeling. Several times the door would open, and we would all look up expectantly, but it was always a different nurse with news about some other patient. One time, the news hadn't been good; they called the parents into a private room to break the news, but we could hear the mother through the walls. We later found out a seventeen-year-old boy had been hit by a drunk driver, and his mother's cries still echo in my head. Chloe's mom had grabbed my hand and started humming as loud as she could, but nothing could have drowned out that sound. The only good news had been that Ethan and Lilly had gone down to the cafeteria to get snacks, and when they came back, they showed no signs of having heard anything. Needless to say, the morning was horrible, but we made it, and I guess no news is better than bad news.

The sun slowly starts to rise, trying its best to fight off the remaining rain clouds and casting a warm glow throughout the otherwise cold room. By now my gut is twisting in knots again, my nerves feel shot and the coffee I'm holding probably isn't helping. What number is it now, four? Five? I lost count. My eyes settle on the garbage can in the corner of the room. Taking a final drink, I head over to throw it away.

It makes a solid *thunk* as the almost full cup hits the bottom of the empty can. I slowly pull my hands behind head and stretch. All my joints are stiff and fight to unlock, and my muscles feel like they've all been bunched together into a ball. I had just been hiking for several days and then sat in a small plastic chair for several hours, so to say my body is exhausted is an understatement. Unwilling to go back to the chair, I start pacing in front of the large windows, alternating between looking at the white tile floor and the hospital parking lot.

Finally, the white swinging door is opened by a doctor who is accompanied by Martha. Everyone stands at once as the doctor walks into the room. I join Ann as she weaves her way through the group to reach the front.

"Well?" Her voice wavers. She looks tired and unsteady on her feet. "Mrs. Whiteshed?" the doctor asks, tucking his clipboard under his arm."Yes. My daughter Chloe? Is… is she okay?"

"Well, she had a lot of damage to the muscles and tendons in her shoulder, along with the infection in the gash on her leg… plus the broken tibia, the excessive blood loss, and concussion. But yes, she is currently stable." The whole room seems to release a huge breath at once. "She will need another blood transfusion and quite a bit of rehab to regain full mobility of her shoulder, and don't get me wrong, she has a hard road ahead of her, but with time, she should be just fine." A relieved grin slowly spreads across Ann's face and she suddenly lunges for the doctor, throwing her arms around him, wrapping him into a strong embrace. "Thank you so much," she sobs. "You don't know what this means to me. Can we see her?"

The doctor takes a quick look around the room, his face growing stern as he scans the small crowd looking at him. "Only immediate family right now. She's stable, but shouldn't have more than a few visitors." "Of course." She nods and wipes the tears from her cheeks. Turning from the doctor, Ann gestures for Ethan and Lilly to follow her.

I remain standing where I am, watching as she ushers them through the door after the doctor. I turn to go sit back in my chair as Martha walks over to Bill, undoubtably filling him and Fred in.

"Aren't you coming, Chris?" comes from behind me.

Turning, I find Ann still standing in the doorway. "Are you sure?" I ask, the knot in my chest unwinding just a bit. "Well, you're Chloe's family, not to mention a big reason she's still alive. So come on, let's go see her."

I give her a warm smile and follow her through the door after Ethan. Ann wraps one arm around me and one around Ethan and leads us after the doctor. The sight is probably comical to anyone watching her arms reaching up to wrap around the shoulders of two guys who tower over her. Though I had been around Ann for so many years, it still takes me by surprise with how nurturing she is. She's so unlike my mother, who, if the roles had been switched, probably wouldn't have cared that I was missing, let alone stay in a hospital waiting room over night to make sure I was okay.

We follow the doctor down a long hallway with lots of doors. Many of the doors are shut, but a few are propped open, exposing the small room, each with one or two beds. Most of the beds are occupied with heavily bandaged patients hooked up to so many machines, and a ball of dread starts knotting in my stomach. Is Chloe going to look like these people? How bad is she really going to be? Should Lilly be here?

The doctor eventually stops in front of a closed door. "Now, there is something I have to tell you…" he says, turning to look at us. "As you know, her heart stopped once on the way here, but it also stopped on the table as well. She is hooked up to several monitors and oxygen." Ann nods once, her face stoic. "She's also still heavily sedated for the pain and to keep her heart beat regulated. It should wear off in a couple of hours, and when it does, we want to keep her nice and calm. No excitement." He gives us a pointed look and smiles at Lilly before turning and opening the door.

Chapter Twenty-Three

Chris

Once again, the first thing I notice is her face. It is scratched and bruised, but she's alive, flush and looking more like herself than the last time I had seen her. Happiness and relief instantly rush through me, and I can feel a smile break out across my face. After her face, the next thing I notice are all the machines surrounding her. The heart monitors, the oxygen, I.V.s, and a few others, all with Chloe laying right in the middle. Compared to everything around her, she looks so small and fragile. It's eerie how still she is lying. Her only movement is the rise and fall of her chest. Slowly, we move closer toward the bed, careful to not bump any machines or cords. The minute she is close enough, Ann grabs Chloe's hand and holds it in her own, cradling it close to her and kissing the back of it. Ethan moves to the foot of the bed, balancing Lilly on his hip.

"Is Chloe sleeping?" a little voice whispers. "Yes, so we have to be real quiet okay," her brother whispers back, even though we know he could shout at the top of his lungs, and she wouldn't have even flinched. I move to the other side of the bed as Ann smooths back a tangle of Chloe's hair and murmurs to her while tears stream down her face. I pull one of the chairs against the wall over to the side of the bed. Gently, I grab her free hand, careful not to upset the I.V. and let my thumb slowly rub across her knuckles. Silently, I thank God, the universe, and anything else that was out there listening to my prayers for keeping Chloe with me, with us.

We all slowly settle into the room. It's slightly larger than the ones we had passed on the way down the hall, though the reason for that could be that there is no second bed for another patient like the others. Instead, a small sitting area with two matching upholstered chairs are positioned by a small window, pointing to an even smaller T.V. mounted to the wall. A pair of small plastic chairs are propped against the wall close to the bed. I slowly lower Chloe's hand back onto the bed and grab one of the chairs. I carry it to the other side of the bed, and while being careful of several tubes coming from out of the blankets, position the chair for Ann. Ethan takes Lilly over to the small seating area and flicks through the channels on the T.V. until he finds one of her favorite shows. He unshoulders a small bag I hadn't realized he had, and Lilly unzips the bag and promptly begins pulling toys out, spreading them on to the small coffee table in front of the seats. I pull the second plastic chair closer to the bed and sit, taking Chloe's hand in my own. I lean my face down onto our joined hands and look at her face. The flush on her cheeks is slightly unusual, probably the result of an infection. I honestly would have been surprised if she wasn't fighting one after the gruesome nature of her wounds. But the monitors behind her show a strong, steady heartbeat, her breathing is even and easy, so I have no doubt she'll fight whatever it is making its way through her system. I press my nose against her hand and inhale. Most of the fear and anxiety that's still pumping through my system melts away. I know the last little bit still twisting in my gut will go away as soon as Chloe opens her eyes. So until then, I sit here, counting her breaths and waiting for that to happen.

Chapter Twenty-Four

Chloe

Visions of trees whirl in my head. Dark green trees, light green trees, ones that have patches of yellow, ones with little pinecones on them… All different, yet all familiar somehow, though I can't seem to place my finger on it. The part of me in my mind with the trees sits down and looks at them; they're beautiful the way they swirl around me. It's almost like the forest is happily dancing for me. It kind of reminds me of riding the merry-go-round when I was little. When you look out to try to find your mom waiting on the edge, but everything around you is just a blur of movement. You know what the shapes are, but the edges blur. A warm and peaceful calm rushes through me as I sit and watch the trees dance. I suddenly realize why they are so familiar; they look like the ones in the forest I was in. The ones I had been camping in with my friends…

Wait… Where are my friends?

A sense of unease tinges the air as memories try to fight through the trees, trying to tear their way to the front of my mind. I desperately try to grasp them, and bits and pieces poke through the blur of green. But the minute I think I have ahold of them, they slip away, back into the blur. Slowly, the trees start moving faster, just slightly at first, almost undetectable, but then it starts to become more noticeable. I jump to my feet as they rush by faster and faster until the trees become nothing but a solid wall of forest green. The peace that had permeated the air is gone with my dancing trees. The wall is solid and smooth, the different greens now marbled together in the mass surrounding me. I begin feeling like a caged animal, trapped with no way out.

I hastily begin trying to find a way out, but the wall is seamless, with not so much as a crack visible. I sink down with my back resting against one side of the wall, while blankly staring across at the other. A flash of gold catches my attention; it isn't constant like the green, but keeps appearing

randomly. One minute it's in front of me, the next
to the left side, then to the right. I scramble to the
center of the small box the wall of trees had created
around me. With every darting movement, the
color is becoming clearer and clearer until a shape
starts taking form. Squinting at the light, I stand
and can start to distinguish an animal. An animal
with golden fur. Suddenly, I'm running and a
door opens up in the wall of trees, letting me
through. The walls continue into a hallway with
no apparent ending. I sprint as fast as I can and
the animal is running with me, a constant blur
breaking up the green sheet. Even though I can't
make out exactly what the animal is, I know it is
strong. The general size and speed it is traveling
at is astonishing; I am honestly surprised I am
keeping pace with it. In this dream-state my
breathing is still even and clear, despite the fact
I have been running hard. The golden animal
suddenly flashes out of sight, and the hallway
dims without its bright coloring. I look around,
confused as to where it could have gone. I twirl in
a slow circle, and the green wall shows no hint of
the creature. I finish my circle and the animal that
is no longer running with me is, in fact, running
at me.

It appears at the end of the hallway; its long legs, now more distinct, carry it swiftly toward me. Looking at it in the new direction, the face slowly comes into focus. Before I know it, my legs are moving, and I am running right for the animal. As we come closer together, the features of the creature get sharper until I can clearly see a large angry cat lunging at me. Fear plunges through me; no matter how hard I try, I can't stop running at the cat. Like the memories, I have no control in this dream or whatever the hell I seem to be stuck in. A loud growl rips its way through the cat, and its muscles ripple as it lunges at me.

I try to scream as its teeth come mere inches from my face, but before we collide, the scene changes once again. Black, everything goes black. Am I dead? Am I still in that god awful nightmare? I try reaching out, groping around in the darkness, but I find nothing. The only sense I seem to have is my hearing as I pick up a small, constant beeping. It slowly becomes a rhythm in my head. It starts out low and quiet, but the longer I listen, the louder and sharper it becomes. After a while, the high-pitched beeping becomes obnoxious. But as it gets louder, another noise, a soft scratching sound, becomes noticeable as well.

I have been in the blackness for an undiscernible amount of time, listening to the noises around me as more and more noises add to the throng. Once a noise gets to a certain volume, it blends into the background with the old ones, and then a new noise catches my attention. Without really thinking about it, I try to distinguish what each noise is. The loud thud was a door closing, which happens a couple of times. A soft clicking was someone walking across a tiled floor. A soft sweeping was someone rustling papers. But I still can't place the soft scratching sound.

Eventually, other feelings start coming back, and I can feel my body coming back to life. My legs feel heavy, and my arms are tingly, and a slow ache has filled my chest and head. After another immeasurable amount of time, the pain in my head slowly starts to disappear into a smaller throb, and the ache in my chest has narrowed to only the darkness that is my shoulder. The scratching noise from before has since grown louder and more frequent. It is a sound I am very familiar with, but I still can't seem to put my finger on it. Like an itch you can't scratch, it is driving me crazy that I can't remember what that sound is.

The curiosity gets to the point where I just can't stand it any longer; I have to know what is making that noise. I start to struggle against the blackness that surrounds me. I fight against it, trying to grab a hold of something, anything that can pull me from this prison. But there is nothing here, nothing for me to get a foot hold, not one strand of hope. I'm lost in my own mind. I recoil internally, gasping for breath like I had just run a marathon, but of course, my mental struggle has not even fazed my body to do anything but lay here. I focus on the scratching noise again as I wallow in self-pity about my failure to not escape the darkness. The tapping sound of someone walking piques my interest as it gets closer. Suddenly, a sound breaks through that hadn't yet…

A voice. "Hey Ethan, I think I'm going to go stretch my legs and see who's still hanging around."

Ethan! Ethan is here. Wait. Why is Ethan here? And that voice… I know that voice. A warm burning sensation washes over my still body as every nerve seems to come back to life. *That's Chris's voice!*

I love that voice; it's the one I dream about, the one I would give anything right now just to hear it say something else. "Yeah, that's fine. I'll stay here with her."

Someone shifts their weight as I hear footsteps walk away. Another *thud* from the door, and I assume Chris has now left, and the warmth slowly seeps back out of me. The scribbling sound starts up again, annoyingly loud. I know I have heard it a million times, but where…? The curiosity is killing me so much that it becomes an annoyance that keeps growing inside me until I just can't take it anymore, I have to know what that sound is. And suddenly it is there, my handhold to pull me out of the darkness. A glowing light beaming against the stark shadows around me. I reach for it and grasp the light in my hand. Reveling in the warmth that flows over me, I close my eyes and bring the light closer to me, hugging it to my chest. Brightness bursts from the light and washes over me. A relieved sigh escapes my mouth and slowly, I open my eyes.

Chapter Twenty-Five

Chloe

Twenty-Five

Chloe

Opening my eyes is so startling, I have to close them almost immediately. I try blinking but struggle to grow accustomed to the harsh light, but each blink makes more of the memory of my dreams slip away. After a few seconds, the light is no longer burning my eyes, and I can start to distinguish the details in the room around me. The ceiling is tiled and slightly old based on the wear around the corners. Looking across the bed, I can see my legs wrapped in thick blankets. They still feel numb and like they weigh three hundred pounds, and it's doubtful I can even wiggle my toes if I really wanted to. The scratching noise to my right catches my attention, and a small light of recognition blinks from a memory now burying itself deep in my mind. Slowly, and very stiffly, I move my head a fraction to see Ethan sitting in a white plastic chair next to me. His head is bent with his long black hair falling down, covering part of his face. A sketchbook lays balanced on one of his knees, and the scratching sound comes from the charcoal pencil gripped tightly in his hand, moving hastily across the paper. Seeing him draw again makes my heart swell. I can't remember the last time I saw him draw more than a doodle on the side of his homework pages. I lay there for a few minutes just watching him. Occasionally, he blows out a breath to move the hair out of his eyes or readjusts his hand to hold the pencil differently. "Hey…" I manage to croak out, my throat scratchy. "Whatcha drawing?" Though it really hurts to talk, the look on Ethan's face when he hears my voice is totally worth it. His head snaps up so fast, his hair whips across his head, adding to the shocked look on his face. Slowly, his expression softens. "You weren't supposed to be up yet." Though his voice sounds accusing, I know he's joking. "Here." He sets the sketch book on the side of my bed and reaches toward an end table and grabs a small pink plastic cup with a straw. He tilts the straw down for me and holds it in place as I take a small sip. The relief on my throat is immediate as it washes away the scratchiness. "Eh, you know I have always been an early riser." My voice feels better the more I use it. "Where's Mom and Chris?" I ask, looking around the small room and noticing their absence. "She went to drop Lilly back off at Grandma's. She's been cooped up here all day, and she was starting to get restless. According to the last nurse who checked in, you weren't supposed to be awake for a couple of more hours, so that's why she went. And Chris is out in the waiting room talking to everyone still hanging around." Slowly, he moves his sketchbook and sets it on the floor with a *thud*. "Who's everyone?" I look out the small window that's set in the door. "Who isn't everyone? Practically the whole town had been out looking for you, and now most of them are here waiting around just to hear how you are. It's sickly-sweet, isn't it?" His smirk is so him that I can't help but chuckle slightly. "You never did answer my question. What were you drawing?"

Reaching down again, he pulls the sketchbook back up, opens it to the page with his pencil sticking out, and turns it around so I can see the image. "I was sketching you."

And there I was, laying in the hospital bed, asleep. It was so detailed, it had every button on the heart monitor and the wrinkles on the bed; he even shaded on my face where I can only assume there are bruises. "This is amazing," I whisper, fighting the urge to reach my hand up and touch the bruises so detailed, even in shades of gray. "I haven't seen your art in so long I almost forgot how good it is... Almost." The picture is beautiful, yet I feel a twinge of sadness about it, too. The details of my accident are forever etched in paper and charcoal. "Yeah, right. It's just a sketch; it's just something I did to pass the time." He turns the book back around and studies the picture. "No, Ethan. I'm serious, that's really good. You should do it more often… like you used to." "Yeah, maybe." His tone lets me know he wants to drop the subject. We just sit in silence for a little while with just the sounds of the machines around us. Ethan offered to call a nurse in, but I waved him off, not wanting to give up the warm silence for the commotion of doctors and nurses that would soon follow the buzz of the call button.

Ethan returns to his drawing when I start dozing on and off. The sound of the door opening startles me awake. Ethan and I both glance up right when Chris strolls in, looking down at his phone and texting someone. He hasn't seen that I'm awake yet, and a grin breaks out across my face as he walks around my bed until he's standing next to Ethan, who is currently wearing an amused grin on his face. "I hope you aren't going to be on that the entire time; otherwise, I'm just going to go back to my comatose state," I say with mock annoyance and lay back, watching his reaction. His eyes snap up, shock apparent on his face. The phone drops from his hands, straight onto Ethan's sketchbook, causing both of us to laugh. "You're awake?" he whispers, as if he's afraid of scaring me away. Quickly, he whacks Ethan on the back of his head "Why didn't you tell me? How long…? When did you...? Why didn't you get me!" He whacks Ethan again. "Geez, will you stop that! She woke up right after you left, and I figured you would be right back." He motions toward me and all the machines. "It's not like she can go anywhere, anyway." Ethan grabs Chris's phone from his lap and hands it to him.

"No," he responds slowly, drawing the word out and grabbing the phone from Ethan's hand and stuffs it into his pocket, the last text he had been sending completely forgotten. "But it would still have been nice to know."

I smile and look up at him. He looks tired and in need of a good shave, but his eyes shine bright as ever when I look into them. Our gazes lock and all the feelings that have been building up from our separation seems to pour between us. Seeming to sense something going on, Ethan slowly rises from his seat.

"Well, I'm going to go see if the food here is better today. I doubt it, but you never know." He holds up his hand, showing his crossed fingers as he walks to the door. "Warning," Chris calls after him, "it's not." A chuckle and the click of the door shutting is the only response. I break our gaze, feeling awkward around Chris for the first time since we first started dating. I start fidgeting with the I.V. tape on my arm. "You know…" Chris says, moving over to occupy the chair Ethan had vacated. "You really shouldn't play with that. You'll rip the I.V. out."

I sigh and smooth the edge back down. "That was kind of my plan. You know how much I hate…" I pause when I look back up and his eyes are staring straight at me with an expression on his face that is so odd, it stops my whine. "Why are you staring at me like that?" His face is soft with both a happiness that crinkles his eyes and a sadness that seems to settle on his mouth, causing a slight tremble. His wide eyes scan every inch of my face, like he's trying to memorize it. "It's just… I never thought I would see you again, or worse that I would find you dead somewhere on that mountain. The past few days have been a living hell, and now, here you are, finally awake and complaining about a needle in your arm." I look down at my hand, suddenly feeling ashamed. He's right; I put him and everyone else through so much, the least I can do now is not complain. "I'm sorry I didn't mean to be insensitive. I…"

"No," he cuts me off. "You're not being insensitive." He reaches for my hand and carefully takes it in his. "I'm sorry, I didn't mean that to sound so harsh. I meant, if it was hell for me, I can't even imagine what it must have been like for you. And here you are, trying to make me feel better." I shift my gaze from our hands back to his face. "To be honest, Chris, I don't remember much right now. But the little bits I do remember feel more like a bad nightmare than reality. If it wasn't for the fact that I'm laying here in a hospital, I could almost believe I made the whole thing up in my head. I mean, I can't feel anything, pain-wise. My legs feel like they weigh a thousand pounds, and my shoulder feels tingly and bulky, like I have laid here for too long and it fell asleep. Shoot, I don't even have a headache, and it's all driving me insane!" Confusion flashes in his expression. "Are you uncomfortable?" His gaze shifts to the call button. "No, not at all. And maybe that's the point. It's just… I went from feeling everything so vividly to feeling almost numb, like someone gave me a big shot of Novocain. It makes it hard to lay here and have you look at me all sad, knowing that you're hurting and I'm not."

All this talking has made me a little winded and the feeling is uncomfortable. "You only feel that way because of the number of drugs you're on. They are keeping the dosage pretty high, trying to keep you asleep longer so your body has a chance to heal. Now that you're awake, they will slowly start to reduce the amount they give you. But I don't want you thinking about the hurt I'm feeling; it's already going away just sitting here and talking to you. Just having you back here within my reach has done wonders." He gently lifts a hand and cradles my bruised cheek. His hand is rough and warm, just like I remember. I close my eyes and smile, relishing the feeling of having him back near me, too. "When do you think they'll take the needles out?" I grumble, feeling irritable. I open my eyes at Chris's quiet chuckle. He pulls his hand away from my face and covers the I.V. His face softens to the point that there is a touch of sadness back in it.

"Chloe, you were in pretty rough shape when you first came in. Let's just say we were lucky Tom found you when he did, because if he had even been a few minutes later, we wouldn't be having this conversation right now." At the mention of Tom's name, I can feel something, a memory coming forward. Fuzzy at first, but the more I focus on it, the sharper it becomes. "I remember Tom carrying me… He kept whispering that I was going to be okay and that I had nothing to worry about." Another memory floods to the surface, a connection from the last one. "I was being attacked…" More sadness creeps into Chris's face. "How? How did Tom stop the thing? I remember one minute it was on me, and the next, Tom was there." I know there is more, but it has turned into dark a shadow. Any definite details are blacked out, and I search Chris's face, looking for answers.

"We think it was a cougar based on the bite pattern and the way it attacked you. Tom also had encountered one in the woods right before he found you. It must have heard him coming and ran off, then Tom used some quick thinking and used his sweatshirt to try to slow the bleeding so he could get you out of there." Shock radiates through me. Hearing it out loud makes the dreams that were on the border of being dreams a reality.

"Is Tom still here?" I ask, but feel selfish for thinking he would be here waiting. "I just want to thank him for what he did.""Yeah, he's still here. Last I saw, he was in the waiting room. Doctors were only letting family in to see you, but now that you're up, they will probably let a few friends in at a time. When you feel up to it, that is, and when the doctors are sure your heart can handle the excitement of everyone." My whole body would have tensed if the medicine would have allowed it, but since it didn't, all I can do is squeeze Chris's hand and look at him warily. "Why are they worried about my heart?" His face tightens and his shoulders hunch a little. I can sense he was hoping not to be the person who had to tell me whatever it is he's about to say.

"Chloe… your heart stopped twice." He pauses and lets what he says sink in. His thumb brushes over the back of my hand in a soothing motion. "You mean… I technically died, *twice*?" I ask, my voice no louder than a whisper.

"Yes. Once in the ambulance, and once right when they got you in the O.R. The doctors said it was because of the trauma and the shock your body went into that caused it. You were given several blood transfusions and there have been no problems since. But they want to be sure it can handle the stress and excitement of just us before they allow others who may not be quite so… fragile with you." He drops his gaze from my face to where mine laid, watching his thumb trace a small circular path on my hand. I feel like I should say something, or at least acknowledge that he's talking, but all I can do is sit there and stare at the blankets. We sit in silence for a long while; Chris keeps a firm hold of my hand, like he's afraid if he lets go, I'll float away. I don't mind because a part of me is afraid I'll float away, too.

Chapter Twenty-Six

Chloe

"You know," Chris says, finally breaking the silence, "this whole thing has made me realize something…" His tone is serious and the intensity on his face is one I have only seen a few times.

"And what is that?"

"It's made me realize just how much you mean to me. Ever since I rounded that corner on the trail and saw you weren't there… I haven't been able to stop thinking not only about what you mean to me, but also if you knew how much I love you. I never want you to doubt, even for a second, that I love you with my entire self."

Chris and I have been together for years, and we've expressed our love to each other hundreds of times in hundreds of ways, but never have I heard him say it with this much intensity as if his life depended on my understanding of the depth of his love. I gaze down at our interlocked hands, my small one almost completely enveloped in his larger one. I look back into those intense blue eyes, the eyes I had dreamed of looking into just a few days ago. "I know, Chris, and I love you, too. The entire time I was lost up there, I thought about you. Sometimes the only thing that would get me back up when I fell was that I knew you were out there, looking for me, that you would find me, and that you would never want me to give up." I feel my chest tighten as tears flow down my cheeks. This is the first time I've cried about what had happened. Yeah, I had cried when I was out there, but it had always been because I was hurt, but never because of the whole situation, and not because I had been so scared. New tears replace the old ones quickly, and then I'm sobbing... "Hey, you're okay now, Chloe... Everything's okay." Chris gets up from his chair and moves to the edge of the bed. "I didn't mean to make you upset." He scoots closer and smooths the hair away from my face. "It's not you," I whimper. "I...I was just so scared." I turn my head and try my best to bury it into my pillow. Chris gently puts one arm around the top of my head and leans down, trying to hug me around all my equipment and bandages. Even in this odd way, it feels nice to be in his arms again, which causes a new set of tears to start. Chris whispers soothing words to me as the last of my tears dry up. I'm exhausted, but I don't tell him, not yet at least. I just want to savor this moment a little longer. Chris nuzzles his face into the top of my hair and kisses my forehead.

I can feel myself start to slowly drift back to sleep when, as if on cue, the door flies open and in rushes my mother. "Oh, Chloe!" she gasps and Chris slides off the bed. I turn to receive a hug from my mom, her arms gently wrapping around me in a familiar way. "Oh, honey, I was so worried…" "I love you, Mom" I whisper, wrapping my good arm around her as much as I can."Oh baby, I love you, too." She lets go and starts fussing with my blankets.

Chris was right; the numbness is slowly starting to subside. I hadn't noticed it was wearing off before, but now a sharp pain starts to radiate throughout my shoulder. "Mom, how did you know I was awake?" I ask, trying to stop her from moving things around.

"I ran into Ethan in the hallway, and he told me you were up. I also sent him to tell the doctor, so he should be in any minute." She continues to chatter for a little bit, letting me know who all is still out in the waiting room and how excited they are all going to be to see me. The whole time she fusses with different things around me, as only mothers do. The thought of other people beside my family seeing me right now is daunting, and I'm not sure I am quite ready for that.

The doctor soon comes in, thankfully stopping the mother hen from rearranging everything on my bed. He introduces himself as Doctor Thayer. He's about my mom's age, tall, lean, and with a head of dark brown hair that is cut in a military style. He wasted very little time before he picked up my chart from the foot of my bed, launching into a series of questions all of which I try to answer as truthfully as possible. That is, until he puts the chart down and moves to inspect the bandages covering my shoulder.

"And how is this feeling?" he asks, gently inspecting the wrapping. "It's fine, just a little achy." He turns and looks at me with a face that says he knows I'm lying about the 'little.'

"Chloe, you have to tell me if it hurts so I know how to adjust your pain meds." "I know, but they make me feel all weird and numb, and I don't like it. Plus, I just woke up, and I don't want to sleep again." Once the words are out, I feel like I sound like a whiny child. Dr. Thayer smiles and moves over to check my heart monitor. I choose not to tell him about the dreams I was having. Although they had faded since I woke up, and I can't quite remember what they had really been about anymore. I can still remember the general feeling of eeriness I got from them, and I don't want Mom or Chris to worry.

"The numbness means it's working. You need to give your body a chance to heal. Besides, it won't be like this forever; we will slowly start weaning you off them after a few days until you can take the amount at home with a prescription." As he's speaks, he moves from one monitor to the next until he's at my I.V. stand. I don't look as he pulls the needle out of one of the locked drawers sitting next to it. But slowly, I can feel the liquid going into my wrist growing thicker and thicker. I can feel it, cold and tingly, work its way up my arm. As it does so, the sharp pain in my shoulder slowly fades away. My eyes begin to droop. Doctor Thayer nods, then moves over to my mom and starts talking about something, but the words muddle together, sounding like they are speaking under water. Chris moves to my side the doctor just left and grabs my hand. I can feel his thumb trace circles on the back of my hand as I slowly drift back off to sleep.

Chapter Twenty-Seven

Chloe

I am disoriented when I wake up. This isn't the same room I fell asleep in. I slowly look around and am pleased to realize this room is much nicer, and not so cold. There is a huge window much bigger than the small square from the last room to my right with a beautiful view of the mountain. In front of the window is a nice sitting area with a flat screen T.V. that, at the moment, is playing a basketball game. Chris and Ethan both occupy the small sofa, and they are both chanting and moving around like it will change the outcome of what the players are doing. The door to my left opens and in walks my mom, carrying a tray of food.

"Oh good, you're up." I can see the boys' heads whip around out of the corner of my eye. "Yup, I just woke up, and apparently, we are watching basketball." I sigh in the way only females who have watched countless basketball games unwillingly can. She chuckles and shakes her head as she pushes a small table that's next to my bed over my lap and sets the tray down. She then grabs the remote attached to the bed and presses a button that slowly lifts me into a sitting position. "I asked the nurse for it for when you woke up. The doctor says the sooner you start eating, the quicker all the tubes and machines can go away." I look down at the bowl of soup, a thick slice of bread, some sliced pears, and of course, Jell-O. I grab the Jell-O first and earn a disapproving look from my mother, but I turn back to the T.V. and she lets it go. One of the perks of having been close to death, your mother won't argue when you eat your dessert first. The boys have switched the channel to some reality show where teens go wild, but anything is better than basketball.

"I was thinking…" my mom says giving me a glance while rummaging through her bag. "We should probably start on that hair of yours." She holds up a brush, a small comb, and a pair of scissors.

My hair? I hadn't even thought of my hair.

"How bad is it?" I ask, unsure I really wanted to know.

"You look like a bird made a nest out of your hair and then died in it," Ethan hollers from his spot, not taking his eyes off the show. This time, he gets the disapproving look from my mom.

"Well, the nurses were at least able to rinse out the mud and twigs after surgery, but let's just say you lying in bed for this long hasn't really helped the situation much." She moves closer and runs her hand down the back of my head, lifting one strand and basically dragging it all with her. Stumbling around in the rain and mud, as well as my wrestling match with the cougar, made it a complete mess. "You can also thank your friend Martha, who stopped them from just shaving it all off."

I look at my mom in shock. "I'll have to thank her then when she comes by. What do you think, Chris?" I ask jokingly, motioning to the rat's nest on top of my head. I always love putting him on the spot like this, asking him questions he is afraid to answer.

"Well, um… Let's just say you've definitely looked better." We all chuckle, and I give my mom the go-ahead to do her best to work out the mess on my head.

I had just finished eating the last piece of my soup-drenched bread when a nurse came in, asking if I was up for a few visitors.

My mom had just put the brush down from her final pass. It had been easier for her to cut most of it off than to try to fight with all of it, but thankfully, she had saved enough for a cute bob just above my shoulders. My head feels so much lighter that the small ache that stayed in the back of my head from the concussion actually seemed to lessen a bit. Now that I feel slightly more presentable, I tell the nurse I'm up for a few visitors.

The first group comes in within a few minutes. Bill, Fred, and Carly all filter in the door and stand around the foot of my bed, forming a small half circle. Martha, who is still on-shift, promised to stop by later. They stay only for a few minutes, per the nurse's instructions, making pleasantries all with the same forced smile on their faces. The same went for everyone who stopped by they would come with flowers, stand at the foot of my bed, and tell me to get better before leaving with the same smile and all making sure to only look me in the eye for fear of seeming rude. People filtered in and out for most of the afternoon, and by the time the last group left, it felt like the whole town had stopped by. Every free space in my room was covered with flowers, balloons, and stuffed animals with 'Get Well Soon' written on them.

My grandparents stopped by and dropped off Lilly. My mother's parents were loving and scolded me 'for the scare I had put everyone through,' and wished me well with a kiss from each on the forehead. Lilly was delighted to see all of sissy's 'pretty flowers, and toys,' many of which had been confiscated and were entertaining her over by the sitting area. She had also somehow roped Chris and Ethan into a tea party that was supplied with paper cups of water and cookies from the waiting room.

It surprised me how exhausted I was after all the visitors, seeing as all I did was lay in bed and smile. I'm dozing on and off, watching them play, when the door opens again. This time, only one person walks through, Tom.

Chapter Twenty-Eight

Chloe

I smile as he walks in. I hadn't realized how much I had been wanting him to show up until he finally did. "Hey, fancy seeing you here." I grin as he comes to the side of my bed. None of my other visitors had ventured closer to me than my shins, but Tom walks right on up to my side. "Yeah, sorry, I would have come earlier, but I knew you would probably have tons of visitors already." He fidgets, seeming unsure of what to do next. There was an empty plastic chair next to him, but I can tell he doesn't want to sit and overstay his welcome. "Well, I'm glad you did come by. I want to say thank you... you know, for finding me out there. I don't know what would have happened if you hadn't," I murmur, feeling awkward I said that in the right way. "No thank you required, really. I just wish I had gotten there a little earlier. And been able to help more, you know..." He gestures to my shoulder with a sad expression. I can tell what thoughts are running through his head, because all the 'what ifs' are running through mine as well. What if he had found me sooner? What if I hadn't been attacked by the mountain lion? What if I hadn't fallen down that stupid mountain?

I hadn't realized how long we had been silent until a noise from across the room reminds me that we're not alone. Small footsteps turn my attention to Lilly, who is crossing the room toward Tom. She's using our lack of conversation as a good time to try to rope one more sucker into her tea party. "You know what?" Tom says, crouching down. "I would really love to, but I think I'm going to hang with your big sister over here for a little bit. But next time, okay?" She nods as a small smile breaks out over her face, and she skips back over to Chris, who is now feeding 'tea' to one of the Get-Well bears that had previously occupied my counter, though his focus is on yet another sports game on T.V. Lilly glances back at Tom as she picks up her own bear and tips a teacup to his stitched mouth.

"You know, I think she likes you." I chuckle as Tom stands. "What can I say?" He shrugs and laughs. "I'm a chick magnet.""Oh, and I guess I owe you a new sweatshirt now as well," I joke, referring to the shirt incident from before our trip. "Oh yeah, I will make sure to add it to your tab. At the rate you're going, I will have a new wardrobe by the fall." We both laugh, and I even see Chris chuckle from across the room. Tom finally sits in the empty chair next to him and we fall into easy conversation like we used to when we were younger.

………..

Tom stays for a while, chatting and joking around. It felt nice to have a visitor who actually treated me like a person and not someone too delicate to even come fully into the room to talk to. I start to tire out after almost an hour, my eyes struggling to stay open. When Tom notices, he stands from the chair next to my bed and announces he should probably head out. Chris stands and walks over to the two of us, then holds out his hand toward Tom. "I would just like to say thank you again. You saved Chloe's life and for that, I will always be grateful to you. If there is anything you ever need, please don't hesitate to ask."

Tom takes Chris's outstretched hand and shakes it. "There really is no need to thank me; the whole town was out there. It really was a group effort, anyway. We were all out there looking I'm just the lucky one who found her."

Tom says his goodbyes and his departure signals the end of visiting hours. The minute Chris shuts the door behind him, I let my eyes close and start to drift to sleep when I feel the bed wiggle. I crack my eyes to see Lilly scrambling to crawl into the bed next to me. Chris and Ethan are focused on the game playing on the T.V. again, their paper cups from the tea party still in their hands. I reach my good arm out to her, and she gingerly makes her way over and snuggles up against my right side. I look at the small face staring up at me, her features so much like my dad's. "How are you doing, little bug?" I ask her. I can only imagine what all of this must be like for a little kid. "I'm okay, now that you're back. I missed you." She snuggles her face into me, and I don't even mind the slight twinge of pain it causes. "I missed you, too." I kiss the top of her blonde head before closing my eyes again and drift off to sleep.

Chapter Twenty-Nine

Chloe

When I wake again, it's dark outside as well as in the room. Lilly is still nestled beside me, fast asleep, locks of hair spreading across her face. I glance around the room and find Chris asleep in the chair beside me, my mother asleep on a small cot that was brought in sometime while I was out, and Ethan zonked out on the couch.

Slowly, I become aware of the culprit that woke me up. A slight throbbing has started in my shoulder and is slowly making its way down my arm. A sharp itching is also raking in even lines down my back, presumably from the stitches they used to close up the claw marks the cougar had caused when he first tackled me. Thanks to the numbness of the pain meds from surgery, I had yet to feel them until now. I want to call the nurse in, but I glance around the room again; everyone looks so peaceful, and they definitely all deserve some sleep after the whole ordeal I just put them all through. I try closing my eyes again and focus on going back to sleep.

It's not that bad, it's not that bad, I chant in my head as the throb gradually increases to a sharp pain shooting up and down my arm. I open my eyes again and try taking a few deep breaths and slightly adjust my position. But the pain just keeps on getting worse until I can't take it any longer, and I hit the call button next to me. A quite buzzing noise sounds through the room, and I look around but no one has stirred. Good. A few seconds later, my door cracks open and a nurse slips in. As she gets closer, her form becomes more familiar. "Martha?" I whisper. "Hey, Chloe. Believe it or not, you were actually next on my post O.P. rounds to come check on." She moves over to the monitors and starts jotting things down on the clipboard she has snagged off the rail of my bed. "So, you buzzed?" she asks. "Yeah, my shoulder is killing me. It wasn't so bad when I first woke up, but now it's like a stabbing pain going up and down." I try to motion with my free hand without disturbing Lilly.

Martha turns to the nightstand beside my bed and turns the small lamp on. The only one the soft yellow glow disturbs is my sister, who just buries her face more into my side but her small movement makes me grind my teeth. Martha moves and inspects my bandages, lifting some of them just enough to peek at the wound underneath. "Well, the good news is it doesn't look like you've torn any stitches. But the bad news is your wound looks a little inflamed, and you're currently maxed out on your pain meds right now. I can talk to your doctor in the morning and let him know, but for now, the only thing I can administer is a slight sedative. It will help you sleep, but if I give you anything else now, you won't be able to take anything in the morning." I sigh and give a small nod, and Martha turns to the locked drawer Doctor Thayer had been in earlier and pulls out a small vial of clear liquid and a syringe. "I'm just going to inject it straight into your I.V." She moves back toward me, the syringe now partially filled. She slowly injects it into the tube, and I can instantly feel my eyes grow heavier as the tingly chill fills my arm again. I can hear Martha go back to scribbling on the clipboard as I sink into unconsciousness once again.

Chapter Thirty

Chris

I anxiously pace outside the door, wishing I could be in there with her. This morning when we had woken up, Chloe had spiked a fever. Most likely sometime early this morning in between the nurse checks. Her face was flush, and a fine sheen of sweat was visible on her forehead. She kept insisting she was fine, but we called the doctor in anyway. Afraid her wound had become infected, the doctor had requested for everyone to wait outside while he did his exam. If it wasn't for the fever causing the color on her cheeks, I'm sure Chloe would have gone pale based on the look of fear on her face. I had squeezed her leg and told her I would be right outside if she needed me before I followed her mom and siblings out of the room.

That had been almost a half an hour ago, and the doctor hasn't come out yet. After almost forty-five minutes, the door finally opens. Dr. Thayer steps out and shuts the door behind him. "So, it looks like she is trying to fight off another infection. I'm not completely shocked. While we cleaned the wounds thoroughly when she came in, but we have no idea what made its way into her system prior to that."

"Is she going to be okay?" Ann asks, a hint of panic evident in her voice.

"She should be, yes. I've started her on a stronger antibiotic than we had her on originally. This is just her body's way of fighting off what's not supposed to be there. But I am going to have a nurse check on her more frequently to make sure her fever doesn't spike too high."

Before we can ask anything more, the pager attached to Dr. Thayer's hip starts beeping. "If you'll excuse me…" he says as he turns to hurry down the hall. As we walk back into the room, I can hear Chloe in her best 'I told you so' voice tell her mother that there was nothing to worry about. I resume my normal spot in the chair next to her bed, and she rests her hand in mine automatically though her touch is slightly warmer than usual.

Even though her body temperature is hovering around one hundred- and three-degrees, Chloe keeps insisting she's cold. The nurse said this was also a normal part of a fever, so we spent most of the day rotating blankets on and off the bed. Chloe sleeps for most of the day, and the day after, and when she is awake, she never complains. Every day, twice a day, a team of nurses come in to clean and redress her wounds. Those few occasions are the only times I leave Chloe's room. Though there isn't any part of Chloe I haven't seen before, and I am a paramedic, the nurses refuse to let me stay in the room with her, even though she insisted there was no reason I shouldn't be in there with her. But they just said I'd be in the way, so, I leave and pace outside in the hall until they are done. Even though the checks always exhaust her that doesn't stop her from questioning me about returning to work. I inform her that the chief had given me a temporary leave while she's in the hospital, and I plan to return once she's home and settled.

Chloe's fever finally breaks around mid-afternoon on the third day which was also the one-week mark of Chloe's hospital stay. Today the doctor is going to do another full exam to determine when she can finally go home.

"Are you excited to see if you can go home today?" Ann asks as she fusses with one of the flower arrangements on the counter.

"I am, but I don't want to get my hopes up just yet. He could still say no," Chloe responds, looking at all of us. As if reminding us to not get our hopes up, either.

"Well, I don't see why he would. The nurses say your wounds are healing up nicely, and there hasn't been another hint of infection now that your fever is all gone. You are off everything but the silly I.V. So pretty much everything they are doing now we could at home."

Before I can chime in with my own words of affirmation, there is a soft knock on the door.

"Well speak of the devil!" Chloe's mom laughs as Doctor Thayer comes in with Martha and another nurse in tow.

"So, you want to see if you can get out of here? Or do you think you'll miss the food too much?" the doctor jokes as he reaches for Chloe's chart.

"Oh, I'm definitely ready to get out of here." Chloe laughs, shooting a pretend grimace at the remnants of her lunch tray.

"Alright then. Everyone, you know the drill." Doctor Thayer makes a grand sweeping motion toward the door. I give Chloe's hand one final squeeze with one last reassuring smile before we all file out into the hall, closing the door behind me. Ethan and Ann take Lilly down to the cafeteria with the promise of cookies. I watch them go and take my position, leaning against the wall outside the door. I pull my phone out and see I have one unread message from my mom. I open the text and read the small message.

Heard what happened to Cleo, hope you are doing ok

I let out a frustrated breath. Not just a day late, but a dollar and a half short. I started typing a reply.

For the last time, it's Chloe! And yes, she and I are doing just fine. We found her a week ago. Thanks for the help, by the way, really appreciated it… I pause, my thumb hovering over the send button. I take another deep breath and hit the delete button. It's been like this for years and getting mad in a text isn't going to change anything now; it's just going to start something, and now is not the time I want to get into it with her. I tuck my phone back into my pocket and lean my head back against the wall and wait.

Chapter Thirty-One

Chloe

"Alright, so let's begin," Doctor Thayer says the moment the door closes behind my family. One question at a time, Martha starts administering the basic health exam- blood pressure, temperature, heart rate, etc. The other nurse, who I had seen before but never caught her name, works on a blood draw, and I try not to look as she pulls four vials of blood from me. She bags them all up and leaves without ever saying a word.

"Alright, all of those look good. Now let's take a look at the bite." Doctor Thayer sets down the clipboard and moves to my side. With Martha's help, they slowly begin to unbind my shoulder.

At this point, I am immensely grateful for the fact I am still on a small amount of pain medication. I can feel the slight tugging as the bandage pulls away from my skin. I never looked at the bite myself. I hadn't wanted to, but now it's time. I can't hide from it forever, and if I'm going to move past this, I need to see it. I glance down to see the wound that the cougar had left me. I'm surprised to see it isn't as scary as I had worked it in my head, and there are clean little rows of stitches scalloping all around my shoulder. The skin is healthy looking, aside from the little redness from the irritation of the bandage being removed. The one thing that does surprise me is the sheer number of stitches that had been needed. There has to be well over a hundred small sutures keeping my shoulder together. While it isn't pretty, it definitely isn't what I imagined it looked like a week ago.

"It looks really good, Chloe," Doctor Thayer says, pulling my attention back up to him. They are both watching me, their faces calm and calculating, aware of every expression on my face and making sure I am handling what I see well.

"There are no signs of infection anymore, and the surrounding skin is starting to heal," he continues then moves from my shoulder down to the less deep claw marks on my lower back. "These are looking really good, too, not as deep as they were. Since they were such a clean cut to begin with, you may not scar as badly here. And these stitches may actually be able to come out in a couple of weeks. Martha, you can start wrapping her back up." He picks my chart up again and scribbles some notes down.

"Well, that's a relief," I joke darkly, thinking of the amount of scarring I will have on my shoulder. Though, If I am honest, I am feeling a little better after seeing what a good job they had done stitching everything back together. "So, do you think I can go home today?" I try to hold still as Martha places clean padding onto my shoulder and slowly begins to bind me back up.

"I want to wait for that final blood test to come back before I give a definitive answer. But, as it's looking now, I think you may be able to go home today." He smiles warmly at me before jotting more notes in my chart.

"I can actually go check if those results are back yet," Martha chimes in, stepping back from my now fully rebandaged shoulder. Sitting up, my shoulder is so bulky that I feel like Quasimodo. Martha smiles at me before heading out of the room again.

"Now, I want to go over everything with you again before you leave. Your homework, if you will." Doctor Thayer sits in Chris's chair, the clipboard laying in his lap. "Now I'm not going to sugarcoat this, the road ahead of you is not going to be easy. Remember, the wounds need to be cleaned just like they were here, twice a day. I want you back in here for a follow up in one week so we can make sure everything is healing as it's supposed to. We are also going to give you your last rabies shot at that appointment I have your third one here, which I'll administer before I finish up."

I grimace at the thought of the shot. I heard they were anything but fun; thankfully, I had been out of it for my first and second dose. But since the cougar that had attacked me had yet to be caught, we still had no idea why it had acted so out of character. So, it was better safe than sorry.

"I'm writing you a prescription for your pain medication to take home. My goal is to ease you off as soon as possible, so try taking it in the morning and at night for a few days, then try pulling back to just at night, and then none at all." His voice is firm at this point, and I nod to confirm that I am listening. "Alright, as soon as your shoulder wounds close and we remove the stitches, I want you to meet with Adam Bail, who is a great physical therapist. I have already sent your chart to him, and he will reach out to you in a few days to introduce himself. We have worked out a rehab regimen for you to get your shoulder and leg back in order. Our goal is full recovery on the leg as the break, though severe, didn't cause too much damage to the surrounding muscle. And we are going for roughly eighty percent mobility to return for the shoulder. But I have no doubt in my mind that it is possible for a full recovery, if you work hard and listen to Adam."

All I can do is nod again, showing that I heard him. The thought of never getting full usage of my shoulder back is a tough pill to swallow. Not to mention now every time the weather gets warm, I will have a constant visual reminder of the horror I experienced imprinted for all to see on my shoulder. I may never be able to play volleyball again, though with the tank-top-style jersey I usually sport whenever I play, I might not want to, anyway.

"I know this sounds like a lot, but don't worry, I will go through all of this with Chris and your mom, too. And with that, don't forget you have a team on your side Chloe. Rely on them. You are going to need their help through this recovery."

A soft knock on the door signals Martha's return. She pushes the wooden door open and strides inside. "Here you go, doctor." Martha produces a small manila envelope I am assuming holds the results of my blood tests. Doctor Thayer opens the envelope and pulls out a sheet of paper, and starts reading.

"Well, your white count has normalized, and there is no longer any sign of infection." He scans a few more rows.

"So...?" I ask, looking at him expectantly.

"So," he replies, tucking the sheet of paper into my chart and looks up at me. "I think it's time we get those discharge papers."

"Yes!" I make a fist with my good hand and pump my arm triumphantly. I laugh and glance up at Martha, who does a happy dance with me. Doctor Thayer chuckles at us and hands Martha my chart.

"Go ahead and get the papers so we can get some final signatures. I'll let Chris know, as I am sure he is waiting outside, as always." He gives me a final smile before he turns to leave.

"Thank you so much, doctor, for everything"

He pauses with his hand on the door handle. "Absolutely." He nods and pulls the door open, then steps out with Martha right behind him. I sit back in my bed, feeling nervous and excited all at the same time. I feel as if a chapter of my life is now coming to a close. A very short, but very intense chapter.

Chapter Thirty-Two

Chloe

"Alright, I think that does it."

My mom stands back up from her crouch by my feet. "I can't even remember the last time I had to tie your shoes. Or you know, shoe." She giggles.

I glance down and can't help but chuckle at the stark contrast between the dark blue Converse on one foot and the bright white newness of the cast covering me from toes to mid-thigh on the other.

"Well, you better get used to it." I laugh back. After Doctor Thayer's announcement, I had wasted no time at all trying to get out. As soon as everyone had come back, and I got to share the good news. I had Ethan and Lilly take all the flowers from my shelves and deliver them to the nurses' station so they could be delivered to other patients. Many of the stuffed animals were also taken to the children's ward, though Lilly's bag looked suspiciously fuller when she went to leave, and I could have sworn I saw a fuzzy paw poking out of the zipper. I then sent Chris to go get a wheelchair so Mom could help me get dressed.

Which had been a feat in itself. With my arm completely bandaged and in a new sling, and my leg in a full cast, it had made getting clothes on practically impossible. Luckily, Mom had thought of this when she had packed my 'leaving the hospital bag.' Her creative solution was a pair of black leggings with one leg cut off, a stretchy tank top, and my favorite worn-in sneakers, all of which made it easy for her to pull everything on me with little to no help on my part.

My stomach rolled with nerves and excitement at the thought that I would be going home. Soon, this whole thing would be behind me. Aside from some scarring, it would be like this whole thing had just been a really bad dream. The rush of emotions has my lip quivering.

"What's wrong, sweetie?" my mom asks, stroking my hair.

"Nothing. I'm just ready to be home." I can feel tears pricking at the corner of my eyes, burning at the edges as I fight to keep them in.

"Oh, honey…" Mom gingerly pulls me into her arms. I can feel the tears spill over and run down my cheeks. This has been the first time my mom has really been able to hug me without trying to navigate around wires, and tubes. I hadn't realized how much I had needed it until I was in her arms. Soon, I am sobbing into her shoulder as she murmurs into my hair, carefully patting my good shoulder.

Eventually, the tears stop, and I pull back from her. "I love you, Mom," I croak out. I rub my cheeks with the back of my hand, wiping the last few tears away.

"Oh, Chloe, I love you, too." I can see her eyes are red and her cheeks shine from the few tears that had slipped down her face.

We are both sniffing when Chris comes in pushing a traditional black hospital wheelchair, we had to borrow from the rehab clinic downstairs. The sight of it instantly makes me start laughing.

"I can't believe I have to ride in that thing." The whole contraption looks like it had just rolled off the set of *E.R.* Under Doctor Thayer's orders, I am to put no weight on my leg until the cast comes off, and with my arm in the sling, crutches are completely out of the question.

"Hey, it's only for a few weeks until the cast comes off your leg. It's not that bad," Chris says in the wheelchair's defense. Unfortunately, right then, the front wheel creaks and spins out of control, causing Chris to have to shake it to get it back in the right direction. "Well, it's better than being stuck at home at least."

"You've got me there." I sigh as I hop over to the chair with my mom's help, supporting my weight as best she can. The small movement is painful, and the pressure in my cast causes the setting bone to ache. I grit my teeth as I ease into the seat and wait as Chris bends to adjust the foot holder. Gently, he lifts the casted foot and settles it onto the footrest. I am grateful in this moment for the hospital pain meds they had given me before removing the I.V. but even with it, I have to blow out a long steadying breath and wait for the dull pain to subside. Chris leans forward and kisses me before standing back up and grabbing the handles of the wheelchair. He slowly starts to navigate me out of the room that I have gotten to know so well and down the hall.

I smile and wave at the ladies at the nurses' station, who all smile warmly and wave back at me. We pass Martha in the hall, and she stoops down to give me a hug. "I'll stop by to visit once you get all settled. Okay?"

"Sounds perfect." I smile and she waves before ducking into another patient's room.

After a short elevator ride, our little procession slowly makes its way to the hospital's large lobby. Through the sliding glass doors, I can see my mom's minivan waiting out front. Ethan has it idling up close to the wheelchair ramp and the side door is propped open while he entertains Lilly in her car seat.

He looks up when the hospital doors open. Noticing us, he hops down and opens the passenger door. The bucket seat has been pushed all the way back so my leg can be comfortably outstretched. Chris navigates the chair and locks it into place so it is easy for me to just stand, turn, and slide into the car. He then swiftly collapses the wheelchair and moves to stash it in the trunk of the van. As soon as he is out of the way, Ethan grabs the seatbelt above my shoulder and pulls it down to buckle it in for me. He then grabs the chest strap and pulls it forward enough to slip over my head and tuck behind me, keeping any pressure off my sling. The boys then get into the van and shut the doors. After a chorus of seatbelt clicks, my mom turns in the driver's seat to look at me.

"Ready?" she asks, giving me a big smile.

I smile back at her. "Ready."

Slowly, she pulls away from the curb and starts the drive home. I watch out the side mirror as the hospital slowly shrinks behind us, allowing more of the area behind the hospital to come into view. I can see the beautiful, tree-covered mountains that, even after everything that has happened, I can't help but still love.

Epilogue

Chloe

My lungs burn as I inhale another deep breath. It is a good burn, the kind you get from an intense workout. I pull my hands behind my head, and my shoulder gives a small twinge of protest. A feeling I'm used to and oddly grateful for. It is a reminder to always appreciate what you have and every day you are given. A year ago, I could hardly believe the day would come where I could move my arm at all, let alone have the kind of range of motion required to put my hand behind my head.

Memories flash through my head of the past year. My mom helping me shower, Lilly brushing my hair. Which thankfully, has now almost grown back completely. Chris and Ethan alternated driving me to all my various appointments. My strong support system was there for every new task I found I could no longer do by myself, every tear, every hurt. But they had also been there for every milestone. Chris was there when I got the stitches removed and my cast cut off, holding my hand throughout each appointment. When I started physical therapy, I had four cheerleaders there for me the whole time.

I walk closer to the edge of the cliff and stare out at the view in front of me. Miles of forest stretches out in front of me in a sea of trees in varying shades of green and yellows. A few low clouds float by lazily, and I can see a raven slowly ride the breeze. A pair of hands come up from behind me and slowly grab my waist. I lower my arms and lean back into Chris's chest. The sun warms the exposed skin on my face, and the white scarred lines of my bare shoulder. The first time I forced that tank top over my head, I sat by the front door for twenty minutes working up the nerve to go out and run errands, fighting the urge to change into something that covered up the scars. But once I forced myself out that door, I realized very few eyes actually looked my way while I wandered into various shops I needed to go to, and those that did, didn't linger long.

"It's so beautiful," I whisper, still a little winded from the hike. "Thank you for bringing me here." I had been skeptical at first when Chris suggested coming back to the mountain that had almost claimed my life. It wasn't that I feared the mountain we had camped lower down a few times during the early spring, it was more so the feeling of retracing my steps. Chris had thought it might be good to go back, especially on the first-year anniversary. To do the same trail we had done last time as a way to 'get closure' or so he said. But he hadn't pushed me to do it, and that was one of the reasons I had agreed.

It had been odd to walk past the place I had fallen and see absolutely no trace of the events that had taken place. All the vegetation has regrown, the edge of the cliff showing no signs of anything ever disturbing it. It is almost like the mountain had forgotten, but I haven't. The cougar that attacked me had been tracked and eventually located, and I was sad when I heard it was euthanized. It hadn't really been his fault. I never begrudged the animal for what it had done; it was just going off its instincts. But unfortunately, since it had attacked me, they couldn't trust it to not wander into a camp and hurt someone else. I had heard that reports said it was sick, and that is why it had gone after me in the first place.

"It really is beautiful, isn't it?" Chris murmurs, pulling me back to the present. We had finally made it all the way to the top. This view is new to me, exhilarating to look out over the forest around me. The sun is shining brightly and the birds are chirping happily in the tree-tops. The only cloud in the sky is a small, fluffy white one, happily floating on a breeze, just like the raven.

Chris kisses my head and pulls his arms back. I turn around to see why as he kneels down. Slowly, he pulls a small ring box out of one of his many zipper pockets.

"Oh my god…" I gasp softly as he slowly opens the ring box. The sun instantly glints off the diamond ring inside.

"Chloe Whiteshed," Chris starts, "I have loved you since the minute I first met you and if this past year has taught me anything, it's that I cannot imagine my life without you in it. You are one of the most amazing, one of the bravest, and one of the strongest women I know. And I don't want to waste another moment not being tied to you in every way possible. Because life is precious and can change in an instant, and no one knows that more than we do. So, I guess what I'm rambling on about and trying to say is, Chloe Whiteshed, will you marry me?"

Tears flow down my cheeks as I look at the amazing man kneeling before me. "Chris, you are my rock and my strength, and I can't imagine going through life without you, either. Of course, I'll marry you!" Laughter bubbles out when I see his face light up.

He grabs my hand and slowly slides the ring onto my finger. It's dazzling as the sun-light glints off the center diamond, throwing rainbows everywhere. I slowly tug my hand to pull him up from the ground and fold into his arms. He bends his head down and kisses me so fiercely, I can feel all his love for me behind it.

The amount of love I feel for this man bubbles through me and I break our kiss with a smile. I lean my head against his chest and look back out at the view before me. The clouds are still floating by, the raven still gliding on the breeze; their world is completely unchanged. But once again, this mountain has changed my life forever. The road my life went down to get to this moment had not an easy one; it was paved with blood, pain, and tears.

But even if given the chance, I wouldn't go back and change it. Because it made me stronger, it opened my eyes, and taught me lessons I wouldn't have learned otherwise. And most of all, it brought me to this moment, here on the mountain top, in the arms of the man I love, looking forward into the life we are planning to build together. So no, even if I could go back and stop myself from going down that path, I wouldn't.

I would still walk right into the woods.

About Author

Taylor Rogers was born and raised in Tri- Cities Washington. She started writing at a very young age and entered her first writing contest in the third grade, winning Best Character. Now as an adult, Taylor is proud to introduce 'Out of the Woods' as her official debut as a published Author.

Amy Smull
Photography